The Merman - Bo

Gabriel Braven is a merman, but h

Gabriel should have drowned twice in his life, but he survived. Casillus Nerion, his beautiful merman savior, tells him the reason for this is simple: Gabriel is a merman. Long ago, a Braven ancestor fell in love and had a child with a powerful merman. This child did not inherit the Mer gifts, but Gabriel has.

Despite seeing inexplicable physical changes to his body when he gets wet and having trouble breathing when there is plenty of air, Gabriel's head tells him that Mer, like love, do not exist. Ironically, both beliefs are being tested at the same time, as he tries to tell himself that the pounding of his heart when he even thinks of Casillus is imaginary, too.

But whether Gabriel believes or not, Casillus tells him one more devastating fact: the Mer live forever, but unless Gabriel goes into the ocean with him in four days, Gabriel *will* die.

Can Gabriel accept the truth before it's too late? Can he open his heart to the merman that saved him? Can he believe Casillus' words over their mental link that the Mer will never leave Gabriel? Or will he deny himself Casillus and his true nature until his last breath?

THE MERMAN

BOOK 2: ACCEPTANCE
A RAYTHE REIGN NOVEL
Based on the novel The Sea by X. Aratare

Story by X. Aratare

Cover Art by Mathia Arkoniel

If you would like to see more of Raythe Reign Publishing, Inc.'s offerings please go to:

www.RaytheReign.com

Use Coupon Code 92DDC246EC
and pay only 1 Penny for a Month!

PUBLISHING

THE MERMAN

BOOK 2 - ACCEPTANCE

X. ARATARE
STORY

MATHIA ARKONIEL
COVER ART

Chapter 1

DISBELIEF

abriel Braven stared at the spot where Casillus Nerion had disappeared beneath the waves. There was nothing to show that the beautiful man had ever been there, had showed Gabriel impossible things like gills and webbed fingers, had even rescued Gabriel from death in a watery cave in the first place. But the sea was like that. It didn't show anything at all when it had swallowed people up whole. Gabriel had known that all too well ever since his parents' deaths, when their boat had been capsized by a rogue wave when he was just a child. Gabriel had inexplicably survived the sinking. He had vague, dream-like memories of *something* miles high with tentacles taking him back to shore, but he didn't believe they were real memories.

Is Casillus even real or is he like that monster that I dreamed saved me? After all, Casillus said he's a Mer. A real, live merman! But he also claimed I am, too. That I am "transitioning" or whatever he called it.

Gabriel brought up his right hand before his face and spread his fingers wide. No webbing. He let out a relieved gust of air and dropped his hand back down to his side, but that movement had his wet shirt brushing against his skin, against his sides. Something moved just over his ribs. Something opened and closed, fluttered. Like gills.

No! Gabriel shook his head violently. *I'm not a Mer! I'm human! This is all crazy! Absolutely insane!* But he didn't lift up his shirt to check if there really was something there.

In a daze, Gabriel turned away from the sea and started walking back to his grandmother's house. He knew his grandmother Grace, his best friend Corey Rudman, and Professor Johnson Tims, a professor from Miskatonic University who was running a nearby archeological dig, were all waiting on him for dinner. He had no idea how he was going to be able to act normally around them after this. Because one of two things had happened to him. One possibility was that he had really been saved by a merman and might be a merman himself. Or there was the second possibility, which was that he was really and truly crazy.

Gabriel rubbed his mouth with one hand. The fluttering on his sides continued, but there was no way in Hell he was going to look to see if, like Casillus, he had four slit-like gills on either side of his ribcage. Seeing would be believing and he couldn't believe. He just couldn't.

They shouldn't even be there anatomically speaking! The ribs are like a hard suitcase around the organs. That is the last place gills should be. Wouldn't it make more logical sense if the gills were on my neck?

Gabriel clamped his hand over his mouth to stop hysterical laughter from erupting out of him. His wet shirt stuck to his right side at that moment, and the gills—*no, not gills!*—pushed against the clingy damp material. Gabriel glanced down for a brief second and saw the *rippling* they were causing. He jerked his head up, trying to convince himself that the movement had been caused by an unfelt breeze.

He told himself that the lack of oxygen to his brain from the near drowning had caused him to hallucinate the whole thing. He must have managed to get himself out of the cave somehow and imagined the rest. But Casillus had seemed so real! As real as Corey, his grandmother, or anyone else he had ever met. And Gabriel could still *feel* him out in the water, keeping pace with Gabriel on land. Watching. Waiting.

The dream I had felt real, too, and I know that was just a dream. Yet Casillus' touch was exactly like the man in the dream's.

He had dreamt two nights ago of a lover. A merman lover, if he was being completely honest with himself. He had dreamt of making love underwater to someone that *felt* just like Casillus.

If Corey heard even a sentence of these crazy thoughts he would be saying that this is what happens when someone closes themself off from love: they go crazy!

As his feet pounded against the sand and his grandmother's cottage grew nearer, Gabriel felt the familiar breathlessness he had been experiencing over the past year return and increase.

It didn't use to be "normal." I used to be really fit. But now it's like I'm breathing in molasses. His increased difficulty breathing had to have come from the near drowning. His lungs were strained from that. It had nothing to do with …

Gabriel, you cannot stay on land. The transition has begun. It will not stop.

… anything like that. Nothing at all. He was a Mer? His family had Mer blood? Ridiculous!

If you stay here, you will die.

And that was even crazier! It was always the *ocean* that had spelled death, not dry *land*. His lungs started to hurt as he made it up the dune that lead to the front of his grandmother's cottage. His sides were throbbing. Every time his wet shirt brushed against them they burned, as if something—*the gills, no, not gills!*—was being irritated by the constant shift of material over them. He slowed to a walk and then a crawl as he climbed up the stairs to the front porch.

He leaned on the porch's railing, bending over it as he took in deep breaths, but he still wasn't getting in enough air. His lungs felt like they were filled with sand. Hands shaking, he placed his palms over where the gills would be if such things were real. He felt something move beneath them. He jerked his hands away. His own body was alien to him all of the sudden. He covered his face with his hands.

Am I crazy? Is it possible for crazy to feel this real?

"Gabriel?" His grandmother's voice came from inside through the screen door. A warm light shone down the hallway from the kitchen. "Is that you, sweetie?"

"Uh, yeah, Grandma." Gabriel brought his hands down from his face even as sweat suddenly started peppering his upper lip and forehead. Panic fluttered in his chest. His grandmother couldn't see him like this. He was wet. He was sandy. He might have gills! No, he couldn't have gills. He couldn't! But just being wet and sandy alone would raise questions about him getting into the water that he didn't want to answer, that he simply *couldn't* answer.

"Well, what are you doing out there? Come on in! Johnson will be here any moment," she called out gaily.

He could smell steaks sizzling. The sound of his grandmother chopping something, maybe onions and tomatoes to be roasted, and the quieter shush of the waves washed over him.

"Yeah, Gabe, grab a brew and come sit down with us!" Corey called out as well.

"Y—yeah. In a minute. I'm all … uh, sweaty. I'm just going to grab a quick shower and I'll be right down." Gabriel darted inside and then ran directly up the stairs to the bathroom.

He shut the door tightly behind him and sagged against the

wall opposite the sink. The lights were off, but even in the windowless room he could see a bare outline of himself in the mirror from the light that streamed through the crack under the bottom of the door. His left hand slowly moved up to the light switch.

Just turn it on. I can't keep standing here in the dark. What am I afraid of? A mirror? Myself? Gabriel swallowed. He could still feel the phantom press of whatever it was on his sides against his palms. He shook his head. *I don't have to look at myself at all. Not that there will be anything to see. I'll throw off my clothes and get in the shower. Wash off the salt. Then get dry. Everything will be fine.*

But he still hesitated to switch on the light. His breath came in harsh gasps.

I still don't feel like I'm getting enough air.

A cry started to slip out of his mouth, but he immediately slammed a hand over his lips to hold it in.

Nothing's wrong. Nothing at all. Just switch on the light. Don't look in the mirror.

He flipped on the light, but he didn't honor his promise not to look in the mirror. He couldn't help himself. He couldn't look away. He had to see. He wasn't sure what he expected—or feared—to see. But when he saw his eyes looking back at him in the stark glass, all hopes that he would look no different after his experiences that day were lost. He stumbled over to the sink. His eyes looked *wrong*. His eyes looked like Casillus' had: an iris larger than a human's with a pupil that was far more dilated, leaving only a slender ring of color around the edge. He held his right eye open further and just stared.

Not normal. Not human.

"Oh, my God, what am I going to do?" Gabriel whispered.

There was a knock at the door. Gabriel jumped and clutched at the sink. His heart hammered in his chest and it took him a moment to catch his very shallow breath.

"Hey, Gabe, are you okay?" Corey asked.

10

"Yeah, yeah, I'm fine." But Gabriel knew that he didn't sound fine. Instead, his voice was high and brittle.

"Really?" Corey sounded about as convinced as Gabriel felt. "I can tell something is up with you. Seriously, open the door. You can't hide from me in there."

"I'm—I'm showering, Corey," Gabriel said.

"Since when are you shy?" Corey asked.

He wasn't. Living in tight quarters in the dorm room hadn't allowed for real privacy, not that he was particularly modest in any event. But the changes to his eyes made seeing Corey at that moment impossible. If Corey saw him and noticed something wrong then this would all be real. And it simply could not be real. Gabriel would not allow it.

"It sounds like you're actually curious to see me this time." Gabriel gave out a shaky laugh.

"You're cute, don't get me wrong, but I like the curvier variety of human," Corey retorted.

Gabriel closed his eyes. *Human? No, Corey, I'm not even that.*

"I just wanted to hand you this extra beer I picked up," Corey said. "But if you don't have any need for it, I'll just drink it myself."

Alcohol sounded perfect right then. "Give it here."

Gabriel cracked open the door and Corey stuck one of his pudgy arms in. There was an ice cold Corona in his hand. Gabriel grabbed it and took a deep swallow. He let out a groan of pleasure. His throat suddenly wasn't as tight as the alcohol flowed down. He rested the cold bottle against his hot forehead.

"So are you really okay?" Corey asked. "You sound a little … *off*."

"I'm—I'm good." Gabriel laid his forehead against the door as he quietly shook.

"Did something happen on the beach? You didn't try to go into the water again, did you? Save another drowning person?"

Gabriel stifled another inappropriate laugh. *Another*

drowning person? This time it was me.

"I didn't save anyone today," Gabriel said faintly. *Casillus did.*

"I think there's a rule that you can only save two people a week," Corey chuckled. There was a slight pause before he said in a more serious tone, "If you're suddenly … ah, *not* good, I'm here, you know?"

Gabriel swallowed, realizing that his best friend thought his odd behavior came from being upset about his parents. "Y—yeah, I know. That means a lot, Corey."

"Well, anything I can do, man. Seriously. I can only imagine how hard it is being back here and stuff. You're being a real trooper."

Gabriel just nodded even though Corey couldn't see him. His throat had closed up. He felt sick for lying. *I can't show Corey this. I can't show anyone!*

"I'll be downstairs in a second, Corey. Leave me some steak," Gabriel said weakly.

"No problem!"

Gabriel's heart hurt as he listened to Corey pad away. He ripped off his clothes and turned on the shower. He was sticky with salt. He wanted to wash that off at least. Then he froze, half-in, half-out of the water.

Should I risk getting even wetter? The gills might stay longer. The gills …

Gabriel threw himself into the shower, determined not to continue that thought and even more determined not to consider it further. His skin had been feeling increasingly tight and dry, but as soon as water poured over his body the tightness went away. He let out a sigh and allowed his head to tilt back into the spray. His eyelids slid closed. At first the normal darkness appeared behind his eyelids, but suddenly he thought he saw a flash of light. His forehead furrowed. He opened his eyes to see what it was and the cream tiled wall swam before his vision. The light from the wall

12

sconces above the sink was a steady glow.

Must have been nothing.

He relished the warm stream of water running down his face, throat, chest, and stomach, trickling down the length of his cock. The pleasant heat relaxed his muscles and his lungs. But still he was careful not to let his arms brush his sides.

His eyes slid closed again, and this time instead of the normal black tinged with red he saw a murky blue, like moonlight streaming through water. His breath froze. He was definitely "seeing" something. There were motes drifting through patches of moonlight and down towards the sea floor far below him. He felt his head turn and saw a distant light from shore. How he knew that way was towards shore was a mystery to him, but he was sure it was.

Those are the lights from Grandma's house.

Gabriel? Casillus' warm voice asked. *Are you with me?*

Gabriel's eyelids flew open. He stumbled forward as the world seemed to spin and reform back into the bathroom shower. He caught himself from falling forward onto his face just in time by throwing out one hand towards the wall.

What the hell is happening to me?

He turned off the water and staggered out of the tub. He toweled off quickly, continuing to be careful not to let his palms touch the skin along his sides. But even so he felt a fluttering, felt the skin moving where it shouldn't. Panic rippled through him. He gathered up his clothes and raced across the hallway into his bedroom and quickly shut the door behind him. He could already hear voices and laughter from down below.

I just need to be with people. All of this—this weirdness— will stop if I'm not by myself.

He pulled on the first random clothes that he found in his suitcase as he hadn't unpacked yet. He had a feeling he was wearing all mismatched things, which would make him look more like Corey than like his more conservatively dressing self, but he didn't care. He just wanted everything to be covered. Especially his sides. He refused to look down at his chest at all. As soon as he had a shirt on, some of the tension bled out of his body. He sank down on his bed for a minute, trying to compose himself. He had to act normally once he made it downstairs.

Can I do that?

He let out a soft laugh and ran his fingers through his damp locks, arranging them. He felt the kalish shift against the hollow of his throat. His fingers skimmed over the top of it. The shell was cool and smooth under his fingertips. He slipped the kalish beneath his T-shirt at the same time as his gaze fell on the jewelry box he had found in the basement. The box was on the floor tucked up against the wall opposite him. He stilled.

Samuel Braven called his wife's lover a "thing." A "creature." He also described him as naked, kind of like Casillus was. A scrap of cloth wrapped around his hips hardly qualifies as clothes.

Gabriel slid off the bed and onto his knees in front of the box. His right hand hesitated over the lid. The journal was inside. He could show it to his grandmother. Maybe it would jog her memory. She would be able to tell him that Tabatha's lover was a local fisherman or something. Not a Mer.

Gabriel, can you hear me? Casillus' voice ghosted through his mind again. It was faint. *Are you all right? I sense such fear and confusion in you. There is no need for either. Come to me now and I can assist you.*

Gabriel ignored the voice even though it was kind and warm and a part of him wanted to respond back to it. But he wouldn't! Because that voice would drag him over into insanity, or further into insanity. He wasn't sure anymore which it was. He would have to believe impossible things, and he just couldn't do it. For a moment, he thought of the unnamed protagonist of his own story, who had sacrificed his mind, and then his life, to love a Mer. Was he having some kind of bizarre break with reality like his character had had?

But the gills on my sides are real ... NO! There are no gills!

There are no mermen! I refuse to believe!

Shaking, Gabriel decided the best way to block out this craziness was to join the others in the dining room. He yanked open the jewelry box and grabbed the journal. He would show it to his grandmother. Gabriel got off his knees and hustled downstairs, determined to forget everything that had happened that day in the sea.

Chapter 2

PRETENDING TO BE HUMAN

abriel took a deep breath to steady himself just outside of the dining room. The door to the dining room is closed so no one inside can see him yet. His right hand tightened on the journal. He could do this. He could walk in and be normal. No one would notice anything.

Because I AM normal and there's NOTHING to notice. Everything is fine. Just fine.

His eyes were again "normal" and the gills had disappeared after he had toweled off all of the water from the shower, so there was no evidence that he was anything but human now.

Because I AM human. That's right. One hundred percent Grade A human.

Gabriel closed his eyes and trembled with barely suppressed hysteria. It was Corey's warm, belly-shaking laughter drifting through the dining room door that brought Gabriel back under control. Corey was laughing at something either his grandmother or

Johnson Tims had said. He was being a good guest, a wonderful faux-grandson, and a great best friend. He was being everything that Gabriel should have been, but was not.

Corey would say that I was being too hard on myself. But he would be wrong.

Corey's laughter seemed to reach out to him from inside the room and wrap around him. Gabriel's eyelids slowly opened and he took a shaky breath. The hysterics were defeated for now. Seeing Corey would make him feel better, would make him feel *normal*. Corey always brought him out of his solitary shell and made him want to participate.

We are not meant to be alone, Casillus' voice floated through Gabriel's mind, which caused him to tense up again and his hand to freeze on the door handle.

This isn't real, Gabriel told himself.

But Casillus continued to speak. *The humans cannot fully relate to you, cannot touch your mind and help you bond. You have been trapped, isolated in your own shell, all your life. It has not been good for you. But now that aloneness is at an end.*

I am alone! Each of us is alone! It's a fantasy that we could be connected like you say! And that is reason 1,027 that I know that you are not real! Gabriel found himself snapping. *I know the truth. You are a figment of my imagination! A combination of the Mer I wrote about in* Swimmers *and a dream I had the other night.*

A dream? Casillus' voice held a note of surprise, as if having a dream about him was momentous.

Yeah, a dream. Two nights ago, I dreamed of you, Gabriel told him with a sense of growing victory. *See! How can you be real if I dreamed of you before I met you?*

Casillus was silent for a moment, but then he said, *How can I NOT be real if you dreamed of me?*

What? This wasn't going at all like Gabriel had planned or hoped. He had assumed that once he confronted himself with that point the whole thing would fall apart and the voice would stop, but

17

it did not.

For Mer, dreams are portents of what is to come. You dreamed of me, knowing we were to meet. What did we do in this dream? Casillus innocently asked.

Gabriel flushed hotly as he remembered making love with Casillus under the water. *Nothing.*

Nothing? Casillus laughed, clearly not believing him.

Nothing important, Gabriel answered stiffly. *I'm not talking to you any more.*

Why not? Have I said something to offend you? Casillus sounded genuinely concerned.

No! I mean ... I'm sorry, though why I'm apologizing to myself I don't know. But you aren't real. You're a voice in my head that has appeared because I suffered some kind of brain injury in the cave, Gabriel said to Casillus, though he was really saying it for his own benefit.

I see.

Good.

I see that you have been greatly wounded by your time among the humans and that—

No! No more talking! I'm not listening!

There was a soft huff of laughter from Casillus. *That is all right, Gabriel. I will be here with you all the same. And when you are ready, all you need do is reach back to me.*

Gabriel's hands trembled at his sides. Another burst of Corey's laughter had him balling his free hand into a fist. He plastered a smile on his face, opened the door, and strode inside.

Everything is fine. It is fine. JUST FINE.

"Gabriel, there you are!" Grace stood up from her spot at the head of the table.

The room was lit only by candlelight, which cast a golden glow over everyone in the room. Corey, his grandmother and a handsome older man already had plates full of food in front of them. The older man was undoubtedly Johnson Tims. Johnson was powerfully built and appeared to be in his late fifties. His arms were bulging with muscles that were impressive by any standard. He was ruggedly handsome, with a cleft chin and a shock of salt-and-pepper hair. He had on a neatly pressed pair of jeans with a green button down shirt.

Gabriel realized then that his grandmother was also dressed nicely. She wore a pale blue skirt and a scoop-neck cream colored top. She also had on a strand of pearls that he had never seen her wear before. He felt distinctly under-dressed, though that feeling abated slightly when he saw what Corey was wearing. His best friend had on one of his shocking orange and red tie-dyed shirts, a pair of banana yellow shorts and lime green flip flops. Gabriel's questionable clothing choices weren't that obvious compared to Corey's.

"Yeah, sorry it took me so long," Gabriel said with a sheepish rake of his hand through his wet hair. He quickly dried his hand off on his pants. He feared that any more moisture on his skin might cause a change. How could he explain sudden webbing between his fingers?

I thought this was all in your head? Casillus teased gently. *How could your mind make other people see webbing between your fingers or gills on your sides? This is your delusion alone, isn't it?*

Gabriel flattened his lips and did not respond to those words.

"He had to make himself beautiful for us," Corey laughed from his spot in the middle of the table. He was sitting with his back to the window. Gabriel knew that if it had not been dark out he would have been able to see the ocean over Corey's shoulders. He was glad it was night. He had had enough of the water for one day.

"It's good to finally meet you, Gabriel. I've heard so much about you," Johnson said.

The older man stood up and stuck a massive hand out for Gabriel to shake. Gabriel took it and wasn't surprised by Johnson's crushing grip. The older man seemed like the type that judged a man's masculinity by the strength of his handshake.

"Nice to meet you as well, Mr. Tims—or is it Dr. Tims? My grandmother speaks highly of you." Gabriel was pleased that he sounded so normal.

"It's doctor, but please just call me Johnson. I feel like we're family even though we've just met," Johnson said.

Gabriel gave a tight smile. He didn't let people into his "family" so easily. And though it was petty, Johnson was sitting at the opposite end of the table from his grandmother, which was where his dad used to sit, and that just rubbed him the wrong way. There was a frisson of territoriality in Gabriel's chest.

"I've been quite boastful about you, Gabriel," his grandmother admitted.

Johnson settled back down in his chair while Gabriel sat across from Corey in the last empty spot. He couldn't stop himself from looking over Corey's shoulder at the windows. The glass only showed his reflection. Gabriel imagined, though, that he could feel Casillus out there bobbing in the waves.

Can you see me? Gabriel asked, breaking his vow not to talk to himself.

Yes, I can, Casillus said. *You look tired. Beautiful, but tired.*

Gabriel let out a gasp that he quickly covered up, but not quickly enough. Corey cocked an eyebrow up at his reaction. Gabriel gave him a goofy grin in response. Corey shook his head, clearly thinking that Gabriel was just being odd.

He has no idea, Gabriel thought.

He is human. He can never fully understand you, Casillus said.

That's a conceit if there ever was one. God, do I really think that Corey doesn't understand me? He understands me all too well!

He loves you. That is different than understanding you, Casillus suggested.

Gabriel shook his head to clear his thoughts. He was going to ignore Casillus again. He was going to be normal and participate at dinner. With those resolutions in mind he put the journal on the table. The worn cover looked right somehow in the candlelight. His grandmother's gaze immediately dropped to it. Her eyes lit up with interest.

"Are you starting a new story, Gabriel? I absolutely loved *Swimmers*," she gushed, mistaking the old journal for a notebook he was using to sketch out story ideas. She turned to Johnson and said, "As a librarian, you cannot know how gratifying it is to have a writer in the family!"

"Grace let me take a gander at your story, Gabriel. It was quite *interesting*." Johnson's slate gray eyes studied him over the top of his beer.

"Johnson doesn't like *romance*," Grace clucked.

"On the contrary, I liked his story just fine. It was quite well-written. It was the subject matter that interested me the most, of course." Johnson took another gulp of his beer.

"Because of the Mers' connection to the settlement?" Corey asked.

Johnson nodded. "It always fascinates me how the truth becomes hidden in tales."

"You think there's 'truth' to mermaids and mermen?" Grace teased.

Gabriel stiffened slightly. He forced himself to relax. Surely Johnson, with his gruff, no-nonsense exterior and military bearing, wouldn't believe in Mers! But Johnson did not laugh like Gabriel expected him to.

"I keep an open mind," Johnson finally said.

"Cool. I think being open-minded is the way to go." Corey nodded thoughtfully.

"I like my mermen only in *stories*. And speaking of stories, do you have anything for me to read, Gabriel?" His grandmother looked at the journal expectantly again. "Have you started on a sequel to *Swimmers*?"

"This journal isn't mine. It's something I found in the basement that I thought you might like to see." He slid it along the table to his grandmother. At the last moment he felt strangely reluctant to let it go, as if it would somehow reveal what had happened to him that afternoon. But he didn't stop Grace from picking up the journal. She began to peruse the interior. Gabriel couldn't drag his eyes away from her face. He kept expecting her to suddenly lift her head and say something about Mers.

She's not going to do that. She doesn't believe in them. There's nothing in that journal which can harm me, Gabriel told himself.

You are shaking, Gabriel, Casillus said.

Gabriel realized that his hands were indeed slightly trembling. He clenched them into fists and hid them in his lap. *How can you see that from the ocean? Let me answer that: you can't, because you aren't in the ocean, you don't exist outside of my head.*

I can see through your eyes. That is how I can tell you look tired. You can see your reflection in the glass, so I can as well. You can see your hands shaking, so I can.

You can see through my eyes? Gabriel almost jerked in his chair again.

Just like you saw through mine in the shower, Casillus explained.

That was you?

Yes, Casillus said. *Our minds can become one. Our senses can join.*

I don't believe that. It's too ...

What? Perfect? That is what you are thinking. That such a thing would be perfect, Casillus answered for him. *A connection like that to another person—*

Is a fantasy! Gabriel cut him off. *If you really are a Mer, how do you even know what a shower is? And what about English? How do you know any of this if you're a different species and hardly ever come on land?*

There was a faint chuckle. *I am not speaking in English or in any other language, Gabriel. Our minds are exchanging ideas. I know what these things are because you do.*

If that were true and we are exchanging ideas, how come I don't know anything about you? Gabriel challenged.

Because you have not fully transitioned. This is blocking our ability to join, Casillus stated. *And ... and your rejection of me and your true nature is not helping.*

You have an answer for everything, don't you? Gabriel resisted shaking his head again.

Because this is real, not a clever hallucination as you keep fearing? Casillus said.

Gabriel thought on that a moment. *If this is real, and you have access to my mind, what about ... about secrets? Where does your access stop and my privacy begin?*

Why should there be secrets? Casillus sounded genuinely confused.

Lots of reasons! People have secrets—

Humans have secrets. Mers do not. You are a Mer.

He was distracted from Casillus when Grace suddenly let out a grunt of disgust as she read the flyleaf of the journal. "Samuel Braven. My God, I'm surprised you found this, Gabriel. I thought all of his things were destroyed."

"Why would they all be destroyed?" Gabriel asked, unnerved by her sudden change of emotion. His right hand fluttered up to touch the kalish beneath his shirt. His fingers twitched over the cloth covered surface. He felt far calmer as soon as he touched it.

Her expression grew even more severe as she said, "Because Samuel Braven was a *murderer.*"

Chapter 3

MER BLOOD

"You're kidding, Grandma G!" Corey exclaimed,

his fork freezing halfway up to his mouth. "You've got a murderer in the family?"

"Unfortunately, yes." Grace let out a soft huff of air. She then saw that Gabriel's plate was still empty. "Eat something first, honey. This is not a pretty story and I don't want you to lose your appetite before you even start dinner."

"I'll be all right," Gabriel responded faintly. All Gabriel could think of was the things he had read in the journal about the *creature* and Samuel Braven's final solution. Then he remembered

Casillus' words about why the Mers had stopped watching the Bravens to see if Mer blood showed up in later generations: there had been a great hurt.

Was this the "hurt" you talked about? Did Samuel Braven kill his wife and her lover? Gabriel asked. He knew that asking this question completely went against his belief that Casillus and the Mer weren't real, but he couldn't help himself.

Yes, but Aemrys was not killed. Only Tabatha was. Casillus sounded incredibly mournful.

"Let me fill up your plate, bro," Corey said, and Gabriel nearly jumped. When he "spoke" to Casillus, the "real" world sort of grayed out and he lost track of what was going on.

"Ah, thanks." He gave Corey an uncertain smile. He hoped he didn't look as odd as he felt.

There was a platter of steaks sitting in the center of the table. Beside it was a plate piled high with ears of corn, their burnt husks letting out a delicious sweet, charred scent. A bowl of roasted red potatoes with caramelized onions completed the meal. Gabriel's stomach growled despite the topic of conversation. Like a mother hen, Corey proceeded to take Gabriel's plate and put a thick, juicy steak and a mound of steaming potatoes on it. He balanced an ear of corn on top. He set it down in front of Gabriel like it was a work of art.

Gabriel blinked at it. "I believe you gave me enough food here for thousands, Corey."

"You're looking a little thin there, Gabe. Got to keep you from fading away." Corey sat back down and tucked into his even bigger portion with satisfaction.

Gabriel looked down at the meal. The savory smell of potatoes and onions wafted up to him. It looked delicious, but right then he wasn't sure if he could eat anything.

Do Mers eat meat? What about fish? Or would eating fish be like cannibalism? Gabriel bit the inside of his cheek to stop the hysterical laughter that wanted to flow out of him.

25

We eat many things. What you have in front of you is new to me, though. I look forward to experiencing it with you.

Experiencing it with me? You'll taste the meat and everything? Gabriel asked.

Yes, that is part of oneness, Gabriel.

Don't you find this oneness intrusive? Aren't you sick to death of knowing what everyone else is thinking and doing? How do you keep from going nuts from it? Gabriel couldn't imagine being aware of all of that all of the time. It would drive him mad.

I do not experience everything everyone is doing, not in a direct way. But since I am close to you and wish to connect, I feel far more intimately what you are doing, Casillus explained.

You want to be close to me? Gabriel found the idea of being that connected to someone both interesting and unnerving.

Yes, Gabriel, you need my help. I wish to help you through the transition and take you home.

Oh, right, because you want to save me ... that's why you want to be close, Gabriel realized. Considering they knew next to nothing about each other it made sense, yet he felt a stab of regret that this was the only reason that Casillus was reaching out to him. *Except he's not real. So what does it matter what he says?*

Gabriel's attention was snapped back to the table when his grandmother let the journal fall shut. Her lips flattened. "What a sick, sick man. His hate radiates off the pages."

"Who did this Samuel Braven kill, Grandma G?" Corey asked.

"He killed his wife," she said succinctly.

"So he *did* kill her," Gabriel whispered. Casillus had told him the truth.

It could have just been my mind making a lucky guess! Like Grandma said, anyone could feel the hate radiating off the pages of that journal, Gabriel thought.

Yes, that is true. Samuel Braven was a hateful, cowardly man, but that journal is not why I know what happened, Casillus said. *Aemrys Liseas, Tabatha's lover and your ancestor, told me what happened. All of the Mer know the tale. We share in each other's pain as well as their joy.*

If he told you in person then Aemrys must be pretty damned old considering this happened almost one hundred years ago, Gabriel objected.

He is over five thousand years old. Why is that important? Oh, I see, you think the Mer have a human lifespan, Casillus said.

All right, I'll bite, how long do Mer live?

Forever, Gabriel, unless we are killed by violence.

Gabriel didn't have a chance to be gobsmacked by that answer as his grandmother was talking to him. "You guessed what had happened from his journal alone, Gabriel?" Grace looked at him curiously.

Gabriel shifted in his seat to gain himself time to compose himself, but finally he got out, "At the end of his journal, Samuel wrote that there was only one choice left. I was pretty sure what he was going to do. I'm sorry I was right."

His grandmother folded her hands under her chin and stared into the nearest candle flame. "His wife Tabatha had given birth the week before. Samuel murdered her and then drowned himself. The baby, thankfully, was not killed."

"Holy cow!" Corey breathed, his big brown eyes filled with sadness.

"Are you sure Samuel killed himself?" Johnson's gravelly voice broke the stillness that had descended upon the group.

"Well, he drowned. I suppose it could have been an accident," she said.

"There is another possibility." Johnson's penetrating gray eyes met hers over the table.

"What?" Gabriel asked.

"Murder," Johnson answered.

Or justice. Casillus' voice was grim.

"Who killed him?" Corey asked.

27

Yeah, who killed him? Gabriel found himself asking Casillus.

What was done was done out of necessity, Casillus said.

Johnson leaned back in his chair, his penetrating eyes going unfocused. "No one knows for sure what happened, of course. But there is a rumor that it was Tabatha's lover. A man from the sea."

You guys killed him? Mers killed him? Gabriel nearly gasped out loud.

He was a monster, Casillus answered succinctly.

Thinking back on what he had read in the journal, Gabriel tended to agree. *He seemed pretty messed up in his journal.*

Casillus' voice reached out to him from the watery depths. *Samuel was going to hurt the child that Aemrys and Tabatha had created together. Aemrys was too late to save Tabatha, but nothing on this Earth could stop him from saving his son.*

His son? My ancestor ... this is—this is too much. Gabriel ran a hand through his hair.

"How did you know about her lover, Johnson?" Grace asked, her eyes widening. "How did you know about Samuel and Tabatha Braven at all?"

Johnson's lips twisted into an uncomfortable smile. "I did some research on you before I arrived in Ocean Side."

Gabriel's head jerked up. *Research? What kind of research?*

Grace's eyebrows lifted into her hairline. "Research? On me?"

"On the Bravens." Again, Johnson shifted in his seat uncomfortably.

"Why would you research our family?" Gabriel's voice came out sharper than he intended.

"I had an idea of what we would find when Grace alerted Miskatonic about the settlement," Johnson said.

"What does the settlement have to do with the Bravens?" Corey turned towards Grace and asked, "Do you guys have Native American ancestors?"

"No, not at all. English and Scottish ancestors as far as I

know. Johnson, why did you investigate my family?" Grace stared very hard at the man.

"Not the Bravens *per se*. But we knew about the Mers and we knew that there were legends of them becoming *familiar* with various townsfolk from this area," Johnson explained. "Including the Bravens."

For some reason Gabriel found that explanation wanting in some way. He couldn't put his finger on why, though.

It could be your fear speaking, Casillus said. *Fear that his interest makes all of this more real.*

How can any of this be real? Gabriel asked faintly.

Come to me and I will show you just how real it is, the Mer offered.

I can't ... Gabriel's hands tightened into fists on top of his thighs.

"I see," his grandmother said with a hint of coldness to Johnson. Obviously, she didn't see why he would investigate them for having such a thin connection.

"Forgive me, Grace. I should have said something before now," Johnson said. "My experience has been that people are uncomfortable with our gathering information on them and—"

"Perhaps with good reason. It's a little personal," Gabriel said.

"It's ancient history, Gabriel." His grandmother touched the back of Gabriel's hand. "But I wish you would have *asked* me about my family, Johnson, instead of researching it behind my back."

Johnson held up his hands. "You are right. I should have."

After a few moments of awkward silence, Corey leaned forward. "So are we saying for sure that the Bravens and the Mers are connected?"

At Corey's words, Gabriel's knee thumped up against the bottom of the table. Everyone turned towards him, concerned. He gave them a shaky smile. "Sorry. Just thought I felt something brush my leg."

"It's all this talk of supernatural creatures," Grace said. "You're feeling ghostly touches."

Aemrys' blood flows in your veins. Mer blood. It has passed down through the generations to you. Casillus' ghostly voice seemed to sink inside of Gabriel, each word reverberating through him like pebbles thrown into a still pond.

No, you're wrong. I know you're wrong, Gabriel thought viciously. For at that moment, the memory of his father's death by drowning thrust itself into the forefront of his brain. If there was Mer blood in his veins from a Braven ancestor, then his father would have had even more of it than he did. But his father had died in the water.

"You don't believe in the Mers, Grace? Or is it something else?" Johnson asked. "Even if you think the Mers were a seafaring tribe, why couldn't they have existed up until the time of Samuel and his wife? Maybe even to this day?" Johnson's tone was reasonable, but there was a glint of conviction in his eyes that surprised Gabriel.

Grace crossed her arms over her chest and practically spat, "I don't care whether the Mers really are mermaids or just a seafaring tribe."

"Grace, I didn't mean to upset you." Johnson raised his large hands into the air, surprised by her vehemence. "I seem to be saying the wrong thing."

"It's not *you*, Johnson." She sighed and ran a hand through her hair. "By focusing on a possible *lover*—whether Mer or man— we downplay the very terrible thing that Samuel did. Some people think that since Tabatha had an affair, since she was an *adulteress*, she deserved what happened to her."

"Oh, Grace, no, I didn't mean—"

His grandmother held up a hand this time. "I *know*. But so many have. I just don't want to perpetuate it any further. Not in this house."

"Forgive me. I truly thought you would be *pleased* that you might be related to the mysterious Mers," Johnson said.

"The Bravens have had more than enough grief from the sea," she said. Her eyes flickered to Gabriel and then away.

It was clear that she was thinking of her son and daughter-in-law. Gabriel reached over and touched her hand. She laced her fingers through his. For a moment, he thought he saw webbing between his fingers, but between one blink and the next it was gone.

A trick of the light, Gabriel thought.

You're beginning to see yourself as you really are, Casillus corrected.

"Grandma G said you were in the military before you became a professor," Corey said, changing the direction of the conversation deftly.

"In the military for thirty years. Met some of the Miskatonic folks when I was stationed out East. Discovered we all had common *interests* and that they could use a man like me," Johnson replied.

"A man like you? I would imagine that academia would be boring for someone used to action," Gabriel said.

A slow smile crossed Johnson's lips. "Oh, you would be surprised at how much excitement there can be."

"Well, you do work for Miskatonic!" Corey piped in.

"Heard the rumors about the university, have you?" Johnson's smile was a little more forced.

"Who hasn't?" Grace asked. "It has certainly cloaked itself in mystery."

Johnson tented his fingers beneath his chin. "In some ways, Miskatonic hasn't done itself any favors with the extreme secrecy. But the idea is that people are *safer* not knowing what really is going on out there."

"That sounds like the excuses the government makes for keeping UFOs a secret!" Corey cried. When everyone looked at him blankly, he explained, "It's said that the government has hidden the truth of the existence of extraterrestrials visiting Earth and probing people! They use the excuse that the public would panic if they knew the truth."

"I think you lost all of us at *probing*, Corey," Gabriel said faintly.

"Actually, despite the *probing*, Corey is right.   What Miskatonic studies, for the most part, are things that would cause many people to *question* both the world around them and many other things," Johnson said with a thoughtful nod.

"So Miskatonic is hiding the existence of aliens from us?" Gabriel asked. Though he was joking, his chest was tight.

"Something like that, but if I said more, I'd have to kill you." Johnson gave them all an amused smile.

"Does that go for all the people working for you? A friend of a friend is on the dig," Corey said. "Her name is Greta. We'd like to see her and maybe hang out or something."

"Greta Anderson." Johnson nodded. "She's quite talented, and determined to get on at Miskatonic. Which reminds me. Would you boys like to take a tour of the dig site tomorrow? Greta can join us if you'd like."

"Only if Gabriel is feeling well enough." Grace was giving him a significant look.

"I'm sure after a good night's rest I'll be fine."   Gabriel hoped he looked more confident than he felt. Casillus had gone silent, and even though he should have wanted that, it unnerved him.

"You've been saying that the whole year, Gabe," Corey reminded him.

"I think I'm going to call Dr. Todd tomorrow and get you in for an appointment," his grandmother said.

"Totally good idea, Grandma G. He promised me he would go to the doc's once we got here," Corey said with a pointed shake of his fork at Gabriel. "You've got to figure out what this is."

It is the transition. You are not ill. The land is just no place for you, Casillus said.

And here I was missing your voice. But then you say things like that and I wish you would have stayed quiet, Gabriel teased.

"You do look a little pale there, Gabriel. I'm not much for doctors myself, but maybe you should go." Johnson looked at him with those intelligent, penetrating eyes that seemed to see right through him.

Go to the doctor's? A tendril of panic ran through Gabriel. The gills had settled down since he had dried off, but a doctor's examination might expose both them and a bunch of *other* things. Things like what had been "wrong" with his blood all year. Maybe Dr. Todd would realize the "wrongness" stemmed from Gabriel not being fully human.

I AM human. What am I even thinking? Why am I thinking this?

Because you know the truth, Gabriel, Casillus said sadly.

Gabriel's chest went tight and trying to breathe became even more difficult as he realized he was starting to accept what Casillus had been telling him. He wasn't human. He wasn't human. He wasn't human!

No, no, NO! Gabriel shouted internally, thankfully, but it was only because he suddenly didn't have enough air to actually speak.

You can breathe. In and out. In and out, Casillus' soothing voice rushed through his mind. *Breathe with me, Gabriel. Breathe with me.*

But Gabriel's lungs stubbornly wouldn't inflate fully.

I can't! Gabriel cried.

Everyone at the table was looking at him oddly again. He knew he had to speak, but he couldn't. He couldn't get enough air to form words.

Breathe with me. Breathe with me, Casillus repeated firmly yet gently.

Suddenly, Gabriel felt the Mer's chest rising and falling as if it were his own chest. And then the rise and fall of his chest was matching the rise and fall of Casillus chest. He was breathing deeply, fully, and the panic eased.

"I'll go to the doctor's. Though I just think it's a case of too much sun today and … and stuff," Gabriel got out finally. He sounded breathless, but no one seemed to notice thankfully.

Everyone seemed to relax after he spoke and agreed to their plan. But he had no intention of going to any doctor. He wasn't sick. He was … he wasn't sure what he was.

Transitioning. That's what Casillus said. Gabriel felt like his stomach plummeted to his feet at that moment. He wanted to keep hanging on to his denial like it was a comforting blanket, but it was slipping away from him. *T—thank you, Casillus. For helping me.*

No thanks are needed, Casillus said.

Is this real? Are you real? Gabriel repeated his earlier question.

I am real. This is real, the Mer answered.

Gabriel closed his eyes.

Chapter 4

THE CALL

*D*inner conversation drifted into other subjects that had nothing to do with Mers or the dig at the old Morse place. Gabriel found himself staring down at his plate and hardly listening. Everyone's words just flowed over him without any understanding or acknowledgement on his part. Instead, he concentrated on the sound of the waves and the swish of Casillus' body as he swam in the water just off the coast.

I'm hearing through your ears, Gabriel said. There was a touch of wonder in his voice. He still couldn't believe in Casillus' reality fully, yet he was having a much harder time denying it now. His denials were the only thing that sounded forced.

Yes, you are opening yourself up more to our connection. It is wonderful! Casillus answered before giving a happy kick of his legs that Gabriel could hear and almost feel.

Gabriel nearly laughed out loud. It was such an exuberant

reaction. It brought to mind all of his own forgotten joy at swimming in the water, at being so light and graceful, at being able to express his emotions physically with the soft caress of the water against his skin the only response he needed. He allowed himself to drift with Casillus.

Are you ... singing? I'm hearing this soft hum-like singing. It was a soothing sound, reminding Gabriel of a lullaby. His eyelids actually wanted to close, and he imagined curling up into a ball and falling asleep with that sound in his ears.

I am. Do you like it?

It's beautiful. I can't believe my mind would be able to make up something so lovely, Gabriel admitted.

I'm still not real? Casillus laughed softly, and Gabriel thought he felt the Mer shake his head. *Well, I cannot take credit for this song and neither can you. It is one that was sung to me by my mother and to her by her mother and so on. It goes back a hundred generations.*

You have a mother and a father?

Casillus let out another laugh, this time an indulgent one. *Yes, Gabriel. Like humans, Mers need both sexes to reproduce.*

Are your parents ... still alive?

Yes, as are my grandparents, great grandparents and great-great grandparents. As I said, Mers do not die of old age. Only violence and accidents can kill us, Casillus explained.

So why isn't the sea overrun with Mers then? Why aren't you being picked up in fishing nets? Or found washed up on beaches after a storm? Gabriel argued.

The sea is vast and can hold many of us without revealing our existence, and we are careful. But we are, in fact, few. We do not reproduce easily. It is Nature's way of keeping balance by giving us such long lives, but taking away our fecundity.

Gabriel thought on that a moment. He wasn't sure if continuing this conversation was buying more deeply into the delusion that Casillus was real or not, but he found himself asking, *Is that why you mate with humans?*

Yes, humans are far more fertile and hybrids can be conceived quite easily, but ... we do not do so any longer.

Why not?

The cost of it became too high. Casillus sounded pained as he said this.

What do you mean?

Few children were born that transitioned fully to the sea, and those who remained ashore were ... were in danger. Many humans turned against them. There were deaths. So we retreated, for the most part, and left humanity to its own devices.

Until you find someone like me ...

Yes, and then there is great joy. Another member of our people. Another Mer. Your existence will again raise up the idea that mating with humans is a viable method for us to increase our population.

Gabriel swallowed as he imagined what someone like Johnson Tims or the people at Miskatonic would do if they found out about Mers and their plans for mating. *You wouldn't be able to keep the Mers a secret, Casillus, if you did that now. The human world is incredibly interconnected. One video, one picture of a real, live Mer and it would be on the Internet in seconds and flying around the world at the speed of light.*

Yes, I understand this Internet concept. It is similar to our oneness, but without the physical connection.

Yes, I suppose it is. But more importantly, Mers would be in danger if they were discovered and this mating thing were made known to everyone. People would hunt you. They'd want to catch you, study you. Gabriel's chest tightened at the thought of Mers being swept up in large nets, harpooned, or drugged and then dissected. It was too horrible to contemplate. For as many people as would be awed that Mers existed, there would be just as many that would hate them and want to destroy them. His heart rate sped up.

Be at ease, Gabriel. That will not happen. Mers are not

helpless, Casillus assured him. *We have ways to fight back if we are truly threatened. And, as I said, your existence will only open the doors for a discussion, not force any decisions. Not right now, in any event. Not for some time.*

Right. No decisions. Just discussions and ... I keep vacillating between believing you're in my head and then fearing you aren't, Gabriel confessed.

Acceptance takes time, Casillus responded gently.

Gabriel suddenly felt someone's hand cover one of his own. His head jerked up and he found himself blinking blearily at his grandmother, who was leaning over towards him. He had been so deeply in conversation with Casillus that he had lost track of everything else around him.

She smiled gently as she suggested, "Why don't you go upstairs and get some sleep, Gabriel? You look so tired."

He realized he was exhausted, core-deep exhausted.

"There's going to be a bit of walking tomorrow at the site," Johnson said, and added with a gruff smile, "And the sun can just *drain* you as well. You'll need your strength."

"Don't worry about setting your alarm, Gabe. I'll wake you up in time to shower and eat before we go," Corey said. His round face was drawn into a concerned frown, and Gabriel could see that he had his "worry eyes" on.

"Thanks, Corey. That sounds perfect. I guess I'm even more tired than I realized. Great dinner, Grandma. Sorry to leave in the middle of it." Gabriel leaned over and kissed his grandmother on the temple. He waved to Johnson. "Nice meeting you, Johnson. See you all tomorrow."

"And you, Gabriel." Johnson's gaze followed after him speculatively as Gabriel turned away.

His legs felt leaden as he walked out of the dining room and up the stairs. He felt like he was wearing ankle weights. Gabriel made it to the top of the stairs before exhaustion caused his shoulders to sag and him to lean heavily against the hallway wall.

He had to rest for a moment. His right hand rose up to the top of his shirt and pulled at his collar. The light material felt like it was strangling him. Every breath was a battle. He was actually seeing a few star bursts of white light before his eyes, which only happened when a person didn't get enough oxygen. Panic flared in Gabriel's chest. He closed his eyes and dug his fingernails into his palms. He could breathe. He could breathe! He was all right. Nothing was wrong with him. This feeling would go away.

Let me help you again, Gabriel, Casillus offered. *Breathe with me. Feel my chest rise and fall.*

But Gabriel resisted Casillus' words of comfort and connection this time. *I have to do this on my own! I can't—can't count on—on—*

Why can you not count on me? Casillus asked, and then said with dawning realization, *You fear I will leave you. I will never leave you, Gabriel.*

Gabriel jerked upright. That was exactly what he had dreamed Casillus—or the man—saying to him. *What did you say?*

Breathe with me, Casillus repeated.

No! Casillus, what did you say about not leaving me? Gabriel demanded even as his chest burned.

I will never leave you, the Mer repeated.

Gabriel shook his head. *Just when I start to think you're real and not from my messed up imagination you say—*

Exactly what you have always wanted to hear?

The man in the dream I had said those exact same words, Gabriel said. *After we made ... it doesn't matter. It's just that no one says those things, or if they do, they don't really mean them.*

I say them. I mean them, Casillus responded firmly. *But you will only believe them when time proves that I am not a liar. I cannot convince you now, and your lack of breath is a far more pressing problem. Now breathe with me.*

But—

We can talk after you are steady on your feet. If you do not breathe with me, I will come in the house after you, Casillus threatened.

WHAT?

I will put your back against my front so that you can feel my chest moving, and yours will then do the same. I will come for you, Gabriel, if you continue to put yourself in danger. Do you want that? Do you want me to come get you?

Gabriel let out a breathy laugh. A half naked merman pushing open the back door and leaving wet footprints all along the hall as he stormed upstairs would be quite a sight. Something in him thrilled at the thought. If Casillus did come and he was seen by everyone else then he was real, but if he didn't come then it was all in Gabriel's head. *And I don't want him to go away. Not yet. Not right now.* Honestly, it wasn't all that surprising that he wanted this illusion—if it was an illusion—to continue. With Casillus in his head he truly didn't feel alone, and he was so frightened right now by what was happening to him. He sent to the Mer, *All right. All right. Help me breathe. I'm not going to fight you on this.*

Close your eyes and see through mine. Be in my body, Gabriel, Casillus instructed.

Gabriel let his eyelids fall shut. He saw only the familiar darkness behind them. He waited to start hearing the sea or seeing underwater like he had before. But nothing happened. Once again, he found himself digging his nails into his palms and about to let out a sob of frustration as his breaths shortened.

It's not working! Gabriel cried.

It is because you're holding back, Casillus said.

But I'm trying! I'm really trying! Casillus, I can't breathe ...

I know you have doubts, you are fighting very hard not to believe me real, but let go of that for now. Listen to your heartbeat and you will find mine as well. Casillus' voice was soothing. *I am with you, Gabriel. I am right there with you and you are right here with me.*

I'm afraid!

I know. Imagine my arms around you. I am holding you to me. You are safe. You are not alone. Let go.

Gabriel nodded. Only after doing it did he realize that Casillus could not see his assent, but the Mer must have felt it because he said nothing more. Gabriel found his head sinking forward, his chin resting against his chest, as he listened to his heartbeat. It was thumping hard as he struggled to breathe, but behind his own rattling beat he sensed a steadier thump.

Yes, Gabriel. That is my heart. Reach for it, Casillus whispered.

Gabriel followed the sound of that second heart, that strong heart, until the sound of it completely filled his ears and not even his own erratic breathing could be heard above it. That was when he saw a flash of silver behind his eyelids. He nearly opened his eyes in surprise, but Casillus was talking to him again, soothing him.

That is moonlight, Gabriel. Moonlight streaming down through the water. You are starting to connect to me.

Why was it so easy for me to just see through your eyes before? To be with you before?

Because you were not consciously trying to, Casillus said softly. *You have to accept and want to connect with me now for this to work.*

I want to breathe, Gabriel said with a strangled laugh. *Being with you is a bonus.*

A bonus? That is a good thing, as I understand it. Being with you will be a "bonus" for me as well, but having you breathe easily will be the ultimate gift, Casillus said. *You hear my heart? Now merge your heartbeat with mine. You can do this, Gabriel.*

Gabriel could faintly hear his own straining heart behind the steady thump of the Mer's. He wasn't sure how he did it, but he brought the two sounds together. At first, it was as if one heart had an irregular rhythm, but then they began to beat as one. Gabriel let out a gasp of relief, for as soon as their heartbeats merged he could take in a deep breath again.

Good, Gabriel. Breathe with me. Be with me.

Gabriel sagged against the wall and breathed. His fingers flexed at his sides as he thought he felt water filtering through them, but then he realized that those were Casillus' hands that were waving through the water.

I'm okay. God, I thought ... thank you, Casillus.

Again, no thanks are necessary.

What's going to happen to me? Will I ever be able to breathe easily again? Gabriel felt a spurt of panic in his chest at the thought, but he also felt Casillus' deep calmness. He latched on to that and concentrated on just being with the Mer.

You will when you are in water, Casillus said after a long, quite moment. *Remember how you felt when you were underwater, Gabriel? How light and strong and fast you were? How you breathed so easily?*

Gabriel did remember. He recalled how he had floated in the cave and breathed with ease, as opposed to now. He should have drowned, but he hadn't. Instead it was now, when there was plenty of air, that he felt like he was suffocating. Gabriel's eyelids opened and he bit down on a moan.

I can't believe this is real, Gabriel murmured.

But you do believe. You are just afraid ... and angry. I do not understand where this anger comes from.

I'm not angry. I'm ...

But was he angry? He was certainly afraid. Not being human revealed a chasm between him and the rest of the world that he had always sensed yet tried to reject, telling himself that he was just shy and introverted, not *other*. But being a Mer meant he truly was *other*. Every secret fear about himself was coming true. But the anger didn't stem from the fear or even that knowledge. No, it came from somewhere else. It came from a sense of unfairness and grief. The image of his family's boat sinking and his parents' empty graves flashed before his mind's eye. How could the descendants of Mers drown? How could genetics and the sea be so cruel that drowning ended up being their fate?

I am angry. I'm so pissed that I can't hardly think straight, Gabriel confessed.

I wish I could help you. Perhaps if you told me why you are so angry, I could say or do something to assist.

Gabriel blinked. *You didn't hear my thoughts about my parents, then?*

Your parents? No.

Gabriel realized he had somehow blocked Casillus from knowing this. *They died.*

Casillus' response came after a beat of silence and a sensation like he was reaching out and wrapping Gabriel in a mental blanket. *I am so sorry for your loss.*

Gabriel shut his eyes. He felt Casillus' pain for him. The Mer's weren't empty words. But he couldn't help feeling a surge of angry betrayal when he added, *They drowned, Casillus. In the sea.*

Oh, Gabriel, I—I do not know what to say.

Again, Gabriel felt Casillus' emotions. This time it was grief, and Gabriel nearly shook from feeling another's concern for him. Gabriel swallowed. *Just answer me this, Casillus, how can I be a Mer if my father—a Braven—drowned?*

Your mother, Casillus said.

What about her? She drowned too! Gabriel remembered his mother's determined expression as she had pushed off the boat and started swimming towards his father.

She must have had Mer blood as well, Casillus explained. *Their joined blood is what pushed you over to the Mer side.*

She told me about the Mers the day she died, Gabriel said. *I thought she was making up stories.*

I wish I could hold you, Gabriel, Casillus murmured. *You need to be touched and comforted. I could hold you while you slept.*

Where? In my bed? Or in the ocean? I'm pretty sure you mean the ocean. Gabriel suppressed the mixture of excitement and dread that he felt at the thought of being underwater. He imagined being in Casillus' arms in the black sea with only moonlight streaming down through the waves, turning the water into liquid silver.

And would that be so bad? You can hear the sound of the water around me. It soothes you. Your body would be weightless in the ocean. Your breathing would be easy, Casillus pointed out.

I—I can't do that, Casillus.

Gabriel lumbered into his bedroom, closing the door behind him before he collapsed into bed. Lumbered. It was such an ugly word, but that was what it felt like. His movements were leaden and graceless. His body had felt ungainly as his feet thumped against the wooden floor. When he shifted his body on the bed, he felt like he was flopping about. The squeak of the springs grated on his nerves. Gabriel curled up on his side. His breath came in short, quick gasps. Anxiety began to creep in again.

It will ease. Your breathing will become deep and slow. You are getting enough air. Casillus' voice calmed some of the panic that was flittering through Gabriel.

But the young man found himself asking the Mer, *Am I? Am I getting enough air?*

For now, yes, Casillus answered.

Gabriel piled two pillows together under his head to try to get more air, but that just caused a crick in his neck and his windpipe felt like it was getting pinched off, too. He tried tucking one arm underneath a single pillow to raise his head less dramatically than the two pillows had, but his breathing still felt labored. He would never sleep like this.

If I were to believe you that I am—I am a Mer, how long do I have before I—I can't breathe on land? Gabriel dug his fingers into the sheets and mattress beneath him as he awaited an answer that he was sure couldn't be good unless the answer was "never."

That was not the Mer's answer, of course. *The transition is different for each person.*

But? I hear a "but" in there.

45

But you are older. Your body has been readying itself for some time to transition and go beneath the waves; therefore, I imagine that your time will be quicker than usual, Casillus said.

Like how much quicker? Gabriel took in another shuddering breath that didn't seem to inflate his lungs all the way.

I have never had the privilege of assisting one of our people transition. I cannot guess—

Guess! Gabriel gentled his tone. *Please. Please give me the best guess you can.*

A few days. Four at the outermost before your body will need to be in the water or you will ... will die, Casillus finally answered.

Four days? That was less than a week, and if he was already feeling like this on day one then what would day four be like? Gabriel remembered once finding a fish on the beach that was still alive. It had been washed ashore by a powerful wave. He remembered how its mouth had frantically opened and shut, its glassy eye staring up at him with seeming panic. Gabriel had tried to put it back in the water, but his grandmother had shooed him away from it. *Will that be me? Oh, God.*

Four days is at the outermost. It will likely be much swifter than that. You are already having such difficulty breathing—

But you breathed out of the water! Why can't I? Gabriel was grasping for anything to hold on to at that moment.

We all can for a short time, Casillus conceded.

So I could just go for a dip or something and then come back out of the water and be fine, right? Though the thought of going into the sea, as always, caused gooseflesh from both fear and excitement to rise on his arms, Gabriel would do it if it allowed him to feel better.

Not right after the transition. You will need to be submerged for some time before you can spend any time out of the water without severe difficulty. There was a flash of imagery this time instead of simply words from Casillus. The images were of the vast ocean spread out before them as the sun rose and set hundreds of times.

What would have happened to me if you hadn't found me today? Gabriel asked. He didn't know if that was really what he had intended to ask the Mer, but he found himself truly wanting to know the answer once he asked it.

I hope that you would have made your way to the sea even without me, Casillus said.

I wouldn't have, you know. I really wouldn't have. I would have gone to a doctor or a hospital and they would have found out and—

One of the Mers would have found you, Casillus said firmly, squelching Gabriel's panic-stricken imaginings.

How would anyone have known? You said yourself that the mating—ah, thing with the Bravens happened a long time ago, right? Gabriel questioned. *Are some of you just hanging around this area waiting for people to transition? Are there other people who think they are human, but aren't?*

The connection between all Mers would have drawn someone here even though it has been a long time since we last mated with humankind, Casillus said.

Yet you were close enough to find me drowning in a cave, Gabriel pressed. *Was it the connection that drew you to me?*

Not exactly. I was ... called to be there.

Gabriel stilled. He remembered how when he had stepped foot into the ocean to save that couple there had been a thrum. Was that the call that Casillus had heard? *What kind of call?*

It is hard to explain. It is something that happens to some of us. It is a great ... honor.

Did it come from—from farther up the coast? Gabriel tensed as he awaited Casillus' answer.

No, I—I just knew I had to come here. It was my duty.

Obviously you didn't expect to find a drowning man, right? Gabriel guessed.

I expected to find ... well, I expected to find someone,

Casillus said carefully. Gabriel had the impression that the Mer was keeping something back, but what it was he had no idea. *You must believe me when I say that—that I am overjoyed that I found you.*

Gabriel shifted slightly in bed, pleased that Casillus was happy to have found him. *How long can you stay here?*

I will not leave you. Casillus' voice was certain, firm. *I told you: I will never leave you.*

Gabriel felt a wash of gratitude at hearing those words that he still was too afraid to trust. *I mean, do you have someone waiting for you back home? People missing you?*

Mers are always connected, Gabriel, remember? So though I am here and they are far beneath the waves in Emralis, we are never truly parted from one another, Casillus explained. *So my family and friends are not missing me. I am with them and they are with me. Always.*

I don't know if that is cool or creepy, Gabriel confessed.

Imagine if that well of loneliness in you were to vanish. Would you regret its loss? That is what it will be like for you once you accept yourself as a Mer fully, Casillus said.

But the only Mer I know is you, so it's not like I have a bunch of people waiting for me in Emralis. Is that the name of a Mer city?

It is. It is our capital. But you do have family awaiting you, Gabriel. House Liseas has many members and I know that Aemrys is eager to greet you and help you assimilate. He is coming here—

Aemrys is coming here? Now? Gabriel found himself sitting up in bed as his breathing became strained again. Another Mer was coming here? Why did the thought of more than just Casillus being there cause him to blindly panic again just as he was getting used to the idea of Mers?

Yes, but it will take him some time to get here. I believe he will not arrive until after your transition is complete, Casillus explained.

Or I'm dead, right?

I will not let you die, Gabriel.

48

You'll drag me into the water, then? Gabriel felt a mixture of fear and the desire for the choice to be taken out of his hands.

It will not come to that. You will let go of your fear and anger and come to me. I know you will, Gabriel, Casillus whispered. *But for now you need to rest. I can feel your body aching with the need to sleep.*

Gabriel sank back down onto the bed. He really was exhausted. His eyelids fell nearly shut, but he fought against unconsciousness. His breathing was still shallow, and a tiny flare of fear had ignited in his chest that he would suffocate to death in his sleep. *You will—will stay with me all night, won't you, Casillus? I mean if I stop breathing or something you'll know and wake me?*

Casillus' voice was deep and sure as he answered, *I will never leave you, Gabriel. Be at peace. I will keep you safe.*

Gabriel hugged that promise to himself mentally. He allowed his eyelids to shut all the way and, suddenly, he was seeing the water.

I'm seeing through your eyes. The sea looks so beautiful, Gabriel said, his voice sleepy.

Yes, Gabriel. We are connected. Always. You are not alone. Not even in sleep.

Chapter 5

BLACK WATER

t first Gabriel didn't realize he had fallen asleep and was dreaming when he noticed the hull of the sailboat floating high above Casillus on the ocean's surface. He thought a boat was merely passing over Casillus' position, but then he noticed that unlike the calm sea he had been seeing before, the water was now roiling even some fifty feet down below the surface where Casillus was. The silvery moonlight that had streamed down through the water had been replaced by the hot, white light of lightning.

A storm has come. Gabriel's stomach went rock hard with fear. He hated storms. Storms on the water were so much worse. And to actually be in the sea when one was going on? No. Absolutely not. With that thought in mind, he reached out for the

Mer. *Casillus, you should go deeper. It's not safe here so near the sea's surface with the storm going on.*

Casillus did not answer. A well of unease opened in Gabriel's chest. Why was the Mer not answering? He reached harder for the Mer, tried to *feel* Casillus like he usually did, but the Mer was not there. It was like reaching into emptiness.

Casillus? Are you there? Why can't you hear me?

The storm raged even stronger above him. The water was moving violently even at Casillus' depth. Gabriel felt the Mer being thrown around by the power of the waves. If it was this bad far below the surface, how bad was it up above? Gabriel jerked his head upwards. And that's when he knew he was dreaming. He had moved *his* head. This was *his* body. Not the Mers.

He was underwater and he was watching a sailboat fight for its life against a once in a century storm. And that's when he knew what he was dreaming about. He should have known he would dream of the accident.

No, not this. Please.

Even with the reassurance of Casillus' promise to stay with him always, even in sleep, even in dreams, he should have known that this would be the dream that would come. But Casillus, for all his promises, was not there.

Something's happened. He wouldn't just leave me.

Gabriel looked around the surrounding water, but he did not see anyone else. There was another flash of lightning and the whole sky lit up. It was nearly blinding and he had to blink to clear his vision. His gaze zeroed in on the boat as soon as he could see again. He could tell the boat was already struggling in the violent sea. It was riding up and down on the choppy waves.

Gabriel wanted to close his eyes, to blot out this scene, but he couldn't. His parents were up there. His childhood self was up there.

The wave is going to come. The boat is going to capsize. And then ...

Gabriel started swimming for the surface as fast as he could. He feared for half a moment that like in most nightmares he wouldn't be able to move, that he would be stuck like a dinosaur in the tar pits, but he cut easily through the water. His naked body just sliced through the liquid with ease. He broke through the water's surface, nearly surging three feet into the air above the trough between two waves. His head immediately whipped around towards the boat.

The first massive rogue wave that had capsized his parents' boat was bearing down on it now. The raw power of that black wall of water stole Gabriel's breath. His parents' boat tried to climb the monster wave, but it was simply too steep. Gabriel saw three people, two adults and a child, on the boat, and then he saw one of them—the male adult—*fall* out of the boat as it rose almost vertically up out of the water. The man was his father. Gabriel saw his father's head strike one of the winches on the way down. His head snapped forward violently and Gabriel knew, *he knew*, his father had died right then and there.

But I didn't see this when it happened. I couldn't possibly know that this is true ...

All thought was blotted out as the rogue wave crested and then slammed down on top of the sailboat and Gabriel himself. He was pushed deep underneath the water, deeper than he had been when he had actually been tossed out of the boat. Gabriel's eyes had shut in reflex as his head was pushed beneath the waves, but he forced them open. Above him, hanging in space like an ornament, was his childhood self. His childhood self did not move, at first, just stared up at the upside down boat as if he couldn't quite believe what he was seeing.

I didn't believe it. I didn't understand why the boat was facing the wrong way.

He saw his childhood self start swimming for the surface. Gabriel meant to follow right after, but then he caught sight of some movement by the mast. His head jerked to face it. The mast had

52

been snapped in half. The top half yawned drunkenly away from the bottom half, attached only by a few inches of fiberglass. The movement of the mast was not what had caught his eye, though. Near the mast was another figure. His mother. He opened his mouth to call to her, but only bubbles escaped. She was swimming towards the surface as well.

Gabriel took off after her. If he reached the surface in time, he could stop her from going after his father. His beloved father, her husband, was beyond help. He could convince her to stay with the boat, to stay with him, to not throw her life away needlessly.

This is a memory. Nothing can be changed, a voice whispered. It was not Casillus' voice nor was it his own, but Gabriel ignored the strangeness of having yet another voice in his head and batted it away. He had a chance to reach his mother. He had a chance to change things.

If it is just a memory then how do I know about my father hitting his head? Gabriel thought.

It isn't just your memory, the voice insisted.

Gabriel kicked his legs and stroked his arms through the water. He broke the surface just as his mother started swimming towards his father's dead body. He was fifty feet away from her.

"MOM!" Gabriel screamed, but his call was swallowed by the raging storm.

He took off after her. His strokes were sure. His kicks were strong. He was a better swimmer than she was. But she had a head start on him.

"MOM! STOP!" he yelled. His mouth filled with saltwater and his cries sounded thin and weak to his ears. But he was only twenty-five feet away from her now, though with the powerful swells twenty-five feet seemed more like one hundred.

She reached his father at that moment. She lifted his father's face out of the water and laid his head on her shoulder.

"John! John! Answer me!" she shouted. She slapped his cheeks and opened his mouth to clear it of water.

"He's dead!" Gabriel cried. "Get back to the boat, Mom!"

She didn't acknowledge him. Instead, she was focused on her husband. The ashen color of her face told him that she knew in her heart that he was gone.

"John, *please*, you can't leave me. You can't leave Gabriel!" she begged. Then she swallowed hard and hit his father's cheeks. "Damn it, John! Wake up!"

Gabriel was only five feet away. He was going to grab her and drag her back towards the boat when he saw the second rogue wave coming. His breath froze in his chest and his stomach dropped into his feet. His mother saw it then, too.

"I'm so sorry, Gabriel," he heard her say as she closed her eyes. *"Keep swimming. Please, keep swimming."*

The wave smashed on top of them both just as he reached for her shoulder. Everything spun. Gabriel felt like he was in a laundry machine on the spin cycle as he was tossed end over end by the power of the rogue wave. By the time he was able to right himself and get his bearings, he found he had been sent deep underwater. And he wasn't the only one.

Slowly sinking downwards from the ocean's surface was his parents' boat. It was an almost graceful dive. The mainsail, which his father had never gotten fully down, fluttered as if in a breeze. The ropes for the jib flared out behind the boat like party streamers. And then he saw them. His parents. They were wound together like they were embracing one another. One of the ropes was wound around their bodies. They were falling together, falling into the deep, being dragged to the ocean floor by the dead boat.

NO!

Gabriel raced towards them. The boat gracefully continued its fast fall, the ropes streaming after it. And then his parents were falling past his location. He dove down. One of his mother's arms was wound around her husband, but her other arm was reaching upwards. She was straining towards the surface. Her eyes were open, as were her lips, though no thin stream of bubbles came out.

Gabriel shot down to her and grabbed that free hand. Her hand did not grip his back, though. It was limp and unresponsive in his. She did not blink nor gasp nor register his touch in any way.

Gabriel immediately started sinking with his parents and the boat. He grasped her arm with both hands and tugged, trying to dislodge her from the tangle of ropes that held her captive. But he couldn't break her loose.

Frantically he crawled down her arm to her torso and tried to detangle her chest and legs from the rope by hand, but she was wound too tightly in it. He noticed that the light from the storm had dimmed significantly. He quickly glanced over his shoulder at the surface. What he saw froze his heart in his chest. The surface was far, far away. He was headed towards the crushing depths with his parents. There was a soft popping noise and suddenly bubbles shot up all around him, blinding him. The boat was reacting to the pressure.

When the bubbles cleared, he realized that there were lights coming up from the deep. They were the same ones he had seen the day of the accident and then in the dream of the man. They streamed up towards him. He squinted as they first blotted out the boat, then the rope, and then his parents.

Mom!

He still had a hold of her hand. Suddenly, her hand moved in his. It felt like a flex of her fingers.

Mom? Mom?

But then her hand *changed*. It seemed to elongate. The texture of the skin changed as well, going from soft to rubbery. He felt her hand slide up his arm and something that wasn't fingers wrap around his wrist. It was a tentacle.

The Mer's guardian was said to be miles high ... with tentacles, his mother's voice whispered in his mind.

And I saw tentacles that day. They reached up for me from the deep ...

Gabriel let go of the soft, squishy mass and tried to yank his arm away from whatever was holding on to him, dragging him down, down, down into the deep. But it was too strong. He couldn't get away. Gabriel began to scream silently as the beautiful lights twirled around him and the tentacle slithered farther up his arm, caressing him. The light's brilliance was almost sickening and Gabriel closed his eyes.

Gabriel? GABRIEL! Casillus' voice rocketed through his mind.

Gabriel's eyelids shot open and he let out a scream that Casillus just barely manage to muffle by covering his mouth with one webbed hand. They were no longer in the sea. They were in Gabriel's bedroom in his grandmother's house. Casillus, dripping wet with sea water, was straddling him. Gabriel's arms were flailing above his head as if reaching for something unseen. Casillus used his free hand to grab Gabriel's right one and clasp it. Gabriel could feel the membrane between Casillus' fingers, but it wasn't weird or gross. It was warm and soft.

Gabriel, do you know where you are? Casillus asked.

Gabriel let out a choked cough and nodded. Casillus removed his hand from Gabriel's mouth and Gabriel took in a huge breath. His lungs strained to get air.

"What happened? I was … dreaming," Gabriel gasped out.

A nightmare. No dream, Casillus said.

"You weren't with me! You said you would never leave me! Not even in dreams!" Gabriel heard how accusing his voice sounded and modified it. "I—I'm sorry, that's—"

No, you are right, Casillus said. *I do not know what happened. I was with you and then … it was like a wall fell between us. A wall of black water that I could not breach.*

"Black water?" Gabriel thought of the huge rogue waves.

Yes, please forgive me. I came as soon as I could. No one saw me come. The rest of the house is still asleep. Casillus glanced towards the door. It was cracked open and Gabriel could see the hallway beyond. It was dark, and there was the faintest sound of Corey's snores reverberating in the air.

He shook himself as he realized with growing wonder what Casillus had risked by coming inside a human house. "You came inside my grandmother's house because you couldn't reach me, didn't you? You risked humans seeing you to keep your promise to me?"

Casillus nodded. *I promised I would never leave you, and I will do whatever I must to keep my word to you.*

Gabriel felt like he was about to laugh or cry. He wasn't sure which. Maybe both. That simple statement—whose meaning was not simple at all—had Gabriel squeezing Casillus' hand tightly. The Mer squeezed back.

"Thank you," Gabriel said. "Thank you so much."

Thanks are not necessary, the Mer said with a soft smile crossing his lips.

"You need to stop saying that, because it really isn't true," Gabriel said with a quirk of his own lips.

The pain of one is the pain of all. The fear of one is the fear of all. The loss of one is an incalculable loss, Casillus said. *Each Mer is precious. Every Mer has a duty to one another.*

"Oh, *duty*, right. That's why you're ... here," Gabriel said, feeling a stab of something like disappointment that Casillus' motivation to help was based on something other than his individual worth.

Casillus squeezed Gabriel's hand, smiling. *I am not just here out of a sense of duty, Gabriel. Surely you sense ...* The Mer actually ducked his head, then looked at Gabriel though thick, dark lashes. *Surely you sense that I like you very much. As an individual.*

"I've given you very little reason to," Gabriel said with a faint, pleased laugh. "I've questioned your very existence for most of our, ah, *friendship*."

But you are not doing so now, I see. Casillus tilted his head to the side.

Gabriel looked at their still clasped hands. "You're real. Everything in me tells me that you are. I think I knew you really existed before, but ... well, I can't deny you any longer. I don't want to deny you exist, because ..." Gabriel smiled uncertainly up at the Mer. "Because I *like* you, too."

And what about yourself? Do you still believe that you are human and not Mer? Casillus' stunning blue-green eyes studied Gabriel's.

Gabriel felt the heaviness in his lungs. It was like he had pneumonia. He thought of the past year and all its strange illnesses. He remembered how good he had felt in comparison in the water. And then he thought of how he had inexplicably survived drowning when his parents had not. Him being a Mer made sense of that rather than it being just random fate. "I wish I could just say 'yes' or 'no,' but I just don't know anything for sure. Can you imagine suddenly finding out that you aren't *you* anymore? It's not exactly an easy thing to accept."

You are no different than you were before, Gabriel. You now simply know who you truly are, the Mer said. He shifted his weight lightly on top of the young man.

That was when Gabriel realized that the Mer was literally straddling him on the bed. The damp and clinging sheer material around Casillus' hips did absolutely nothing to hide his beautiful cock and powerful thighs. As he watched, water trickled down those thighs and wet the thin blanket that Gabriel had pulled over himself. Gabriel's cheeks flushed hotly and he jerked his gaze away from Casillus' lovely body.

"How long can you stay out of the water?" Gabriel asked, pretending that the water droplets and not the strong thighs had been the focus of his gaze. The fact that they were still clasping hands was making the deception, if the Mer was fooled at all, that much harder.

Not as long as you need. I will not leave you tonight, though. Only when dawn kisses the sea will I return there. Unless ... Casillus looked at Gabriel mournfully.

"Unless we both go into the sea now, right?" Gabriel shivered. "I can't ... please don't ask me to. I just *can't*."

What happened in your nightmare, Gabriel? Casillus clearly sensed that Gabriel's fear of the sea had inexplicably grown.

"I dreamed about my parents' deaths and—and something else ..." Gabriel shook his head. He did not want to think about the thing with tentacles ever again if he could help it. He was certain that it had nothing to do with the Mers. The tentacled thing was undoubtedly just a figment of his overworked imagination. "Just the thought of going into the sea after dreaming about that is ... I just can't do it, Casillus."

I will need water, as will you. Your breathing is becoming labored, the Mer said.

"Water ... of course!" Gabriel grinned. "The bathtub!"

Chapter 6

ACCEPTANCE

he bathtub? Ah, yes, now I understand, the Mer said with a nod. *That was where you first saw through my eyes.*

"Exactly. I just took a shower then, but there's a pretty big tub in there as well. I can fill that up and we can—ah, take turns being in the water," Gabriel said.

Or we could share the tub, Casillus suggested. The Mer watched Gabriel's reaction to his offer closely.

"Y—yeah, we could do that. I think we'd both fit." Gabriel's cheeks flooded with color as he imagined sitting snugly between Casillus' thighs, lying back against Casillus' powerful chest, and feeling the heat of the Mer's body right along with the water's.

I am glad we will be in water. It will give us a chance to speak more. Though perhaps you should rest. You look so tired. Casillus ran his right thumb under Gabriel's left eye where the skin was softest. Gabriel guessed that there was a black circle there. The Mer's touch was so gentle that he wanted to turn his head into it, but instead he held himself very still so that the Mer wouldn't stop touching him.

"There's this saying: I'll rest when I'm dead," Gabriel said. *And that could be in a few days if I don't go into the sea.*

Then you will never rest, for you are Mer and you will never die.

"Maybe if that's true then I'll try to rest a *little*." Gabriel took in a deep breath. He couldn't quite believe he wasn't human. Not yet. He knew Casillus was real, which meant that everything else was real. But he still resisted thinking of himself as a Mer. Looking at Casillus' beauty did nothing to make him feel like he was of the same species. He found that he couldn't stop looking at Casillus and admitted, "I just don't want to sleep now that you're here."

We shall talk, but if you get too tired then we shall rest. Casillus gracefully swung his leg over Gabriel's body and stood up beside the bed. He did not release Gabriel's hand. Instead, he used that grip to help Gabriel stand. Unlike the Mer, Gabriel's legs were a bit shaky beneath him.

"Whoa! And here I thought that *you* would be the one having trouble on solid land," Gabriel laughed as the muscles in his legs jittered.

The transition is changing every part of you. This weakness will disappear as soon as it is complete, Casillus said.

"That's good to know. I can't tell you how sick I am of, well, feeling *sick*," Gabriel confessed.

You will be strong and healthy again soon, Casillus assured him.

Gabriel smiled gratefully at the Mer. Neither of them moved until the muscles in his legs stopped trembling, and Gabriel felt his smile changing into something else as the seconds passed. Something more intimate. Casillus stood so close to him that he could feel the warmth of the Mer's body radiating down his front. The Mer stood a good six inches taller than him, and his broad shoulders jutted out several inches farther than Gabriel's own. The fingers of his webbed right hand rubbed a tender circle over the soft skin between Gabriel's thumb and pointer finger. Gabriel found himself looking into Casillus' eyes and then quickly away. His heart thudded in his chest.

Love always shows up first in the eyes, his mother had always said.

Love? LOVE? I didn't even think he was real and here I am thinking ... it's ridiculous. Corey would never let me live these thoughts down. Yet every time I look at Casillus, I feel ... I don't know. My heart lifts. My soul shakes a little.

Gabriel cleared his throat. "Okay, I think I'm good to go now. The bathroom is just across the hall."

Without waiting for Casillus' acquiescence Gabriel crept over to his door, drawing the Mer after him by their clasped hands. He peered out into the hallway. Just moonlight and shadows. *And Corey's snoring.* Gabriel found himself smiling at the familiar sound. He had gone to sleep every night to that melody through college, and with a pang, he realized that if he really was going into the sea he wouldn't be hearing it for very much longer.

Shaking the sadness of that thought away, Gabriel whispered to the Mer, "It's all clear."

You can speak to me through our bond again so that we are quieter, Casillus suggested.

"Yeah, I mean ..." *Yeah, I just naturally want to speak out loud when you're in front of me.*

I think I understand. Casillus gave him a nod. *Seeing me and speaking mind to mind feels more ... intimate to you.*

Gabriel rubbed the back of his neck. *Intimate? I guess you're right about that, but I also want to be as precise as I can be. That's easier when I speak rather than just think things.*

Precise? Casillus' eyebrows rose. *Why? What do you fear will happen if you are not precise?*

Instead of answering right away, Gabriel opened the door and stepped out into the hallway. He grimaced as the floorboards groaned beneath their bare feet. Old houses creaked, and the cottage was no exception. He just prayed that neither his grandmother or Corey woke up because of the stealthy noises. He walked heel to toe to minimize the sound of his footsteps as he drew Casillus across the hallway. The Mer did the same.

It wasn't until they were in the bathroom, with the door shut securely behind them, that he had a chance to answer Casillus' question. He felt Casillus waiting for him to speak, but his thoughts were in a jumble. Admitting why he wanted to be precise was part of why he didn't want to just think things, but say them. But he had no choice. Casillus was waiting and he owed it to the Mer to try and be honest. He was glad that he hadn't switched the light on as he faced only velvety darkness. Like Casillus had said, there was a greater sense of intimacy when he saw the Mer while they talked with their minds.

I need to be precise, because ... because I can't control my thoughts very well around you.

Casillus' grasp on his hand tightened slightly. *Gabriel, you need not be worried—*

I do, Gabriel insisted, feeling his chest seize. *The Mer must always be good and kind like you, because I can't imagine having my thoughts open to the world and not being judged poorly for them. I'm good and kind maybe one percent of the time! What about the other ninety-nine percent?*

We are not always so. Acceptance, understanding and tolerance are necessary traits, I suppose, but not perfection, Casillus said in a fond tone. *And from what I am learning of you, you do not need to worry about how Mer will perceive you.*

You haven't seen all of me. You won't like it, Gabriel answered mulishly. He could think of so many petty and stupid thoughts that went through his head every minute of every day. The thought of having Casillus hear those made him cringe.

And if I do not like you, I'll leave you? Casillus' tone was tentative.

Gabriel took in a shaky breath and found himself answering out loud again. "I have this thing about abandonment and speaking out loud helps keep distance between me and … you."

You fear abandonment because of your parents? Casillus' voice was soft, gentle, but the words drew Gabriel up short.

His mind flashed back to his devastation, to the sense of betrayal he felt, when his mother had left him clinging to the boat while she swam out to his father. He realized that Casillus either knew about that or sensed it despite his desire to keep it hidden, even from himself. He found himself confessing, "My parents loved one another so completely that sometimes, when I look back, I realize I wasn't … *necessary*. I was just a moon orbiting them. They were complete together. My mother … she died because of that. She went to save my father. She left the boat, *left me*, to go to him, but he was already dead. She didn't know that, but even if she had, I don't think that would have stopped her from swimming out to him."

That is the Mer way.

Gabriel's head shot up. "What do you mean?"

When a Mer finds their mate, none is as important as that mate. Not even the offspring of that union, though such offspring are beloved.

"Yeah." Gabriel nodded. "That's exactly how it was." He flashed back to the image of his mother and father being pulled down into the deep by the boat. "I just wish they had gotten the part of being Mer that would have let them breath underwater."

Oh, Gabriel …

Gabriel felt the Mer moving to mentally embrace him, but he couldn't accept his pity right now. Not about his parents. It would dredge the dream up again, and he couldn't face that twice in one night. "It's all right. I just wanted to explain why it's so hard for me to get close to people, because they'll leave and I ... I can't bear that."

Suddenly Casillus' other hand was cupping Gabriel's face, and Gabriel was shocked at how soft his skin was. *You paint yourself so harshly for natural feelings. Love and loss, jealousy and envy, anger and joy ... all of these are what make us up and make us interesting. They make YOU interesting.*

But not a nice person, Gabriel responded mentally. He couldn't speak out loud at that moment because fine tremors were running through him in response to Casillus' simple caress of his cheek.

Niceness is overrated, the Mer said, and there was an amused tint to his mind voice. It was something Corey would say, and Gabriel wondered if the Mer had gotten that from his mind.

Gabriel couldn't help but smile, though, and he ducked his head. *Maybe you're right.*

I am.

Gabriel drew in a deep breath. *All right. Now brace yourself. I'm going to turn on the light. It's going to be bright.*

I'm more than ready to see you again.

Gabriel mentally let go of the safety of the dark. He blindly felt for the switch and flipped it up. Warm, yellow light flooded the bathroom. He blinked as the world swam back into focus and nearly gasped when he realized how close Casillus was to him. The Mer's face was only a few inches from his own. This was the first time he had ever seen Casillus in full light. Those stunning blue-green eyes looked even more luminous up close with their larger-than-human pupils. The Mer was still cupping Gabriel's cheek with one hand while the other was holding one of Gabriel's hands.

Casillus tilted his head to the side as Gabriel continued to stare at him in open-mouthed silence. *You are so worried about your thoughts, Gabriel, when your expressions show so much more.*

Gabriel blushed hotly and turned away. "I'm sorry. I didn't mean to stare. I—"

I find you beautiful as well, the Mer interrupted his apology.

A tremor went through Gabriel. He didn't know what to say to that for a moment, then he got out, "See? *This* is what I mean. So much honesty. Nothing's secret."

You did not wish me to know that you find me beautiful? Casillus' eyes lit with an inner glow.

"You being beautiful is a *fact*, not just my opinion," Gabriel said, though his voice sounded rather rough.

Then you have given nothing away at all. The Mer was smiling softly.

"I guess not." Gabriel cleared his throat and broke their physical connection. He quickly kneeled by the side of the tub, turning the faucet handles so that more warm water was flowing than cold. He tested the water with one hand, but he barely registered the temperature as all of his focus kept going back to the Mer who stood beside him. "Let me fill the tub. You should get in first."

I thought we were going to get in together, Casillus said. His tone was unreadable.

A shiver went through Gabriel. "Ah, well, we might not both fit. You go in first and we'll see."

Gabriel hoped the temperature of the bath wasn't too hot for Casillus as he stoppered the tub and allowed it to fill. He was trembling slightly, and he wasn't sure if it was from his usual weakness or Casillus' presence. He stood and backed up until his butt hit the sink. He sagged against it. It was only then that he allowed himself to look at the Mer. Casillus was regarding him quietly.

"Get on in. See if you like it." Gabriel gestured towards the tub.

Casillus cocked his head to the side as if to add something else then. Gabriel almost felt those words about to cross over their bond, but then the Mer merely nodded and put one foot into the water. There was immediately a sense of delight over their bond.

It is warm! Like near the undersea vents. This will be most pleasant! Casillus exclaimed.

Gabriel found himself smiling at Casillus' almost childish delight with the warm water. The Mer immediately put his other foot into the tub and sank down into the water. He put his toes under the faucet's spray and wiggled them. He turned towards Gabriel with a wide smile on his face.

You must get in with me, Gabriel! It is wonderful! the Mer enthused. *There is plenty of room.*

"I—I don't want to crowd you," Gabriel said even though a part of him longed to have water surrounding his skin. His whole body felt tight and dry again.

Casillus spread his legs and indicated that Gabriel should sit between them just like Gabriel had imagined. *You will not, and I see the longing in your eyes to be in the warm water. Come, shed your clothing and join me.*

"Shed my clothing?" Gabriel gave out a strangled laugh.

You cannot get into the water in your clothes. I know this is true among humans. Though humans do wear swimsuits in the ocean, they do not in the bath. Is that not correct? Casillus said. *Besides, you are Mer. Mer do not wear such things.*

"Really? Then what's with the thing around your waist? Is that not clothing?" Gabriel challenged.

Casillus touched the wispy material. *This identifies my House and position.*

"You're House Nerion, right?" Gabriel remembered. "So what's your position?"

Casillus actually lowered his head and appeared almost uncomfortable for the first time. Gabriel was about to retract the question, fearing that even when speaking out loud he had said something offensive, but then Casillus responded, *I am a prince.*

Gabriel blinked. "You're a prince? Like, *royalty?*"

Casillus nodded. *House Nerion has ruled the Mer for millennia. My father and mother are the king and queen.*

Gabriel's mouth opened and closed for a few seconds before he got out, "You're a prince. The prince of *all* the Mer, and you're here, hanging out with me in my bathroom?"

Casillus' head rose up and there was a twitch of a smile on his lips. *It is a wonderful bathroom.*

Gabriel shook his head, stunned at the information. "This is *crazy.* You shouldn't be wasting your time with me! I mean I'm— I'm not a *prince* or anything!" Casillus did that head tilt again, which Gabriel had figured out meant he was confused by Gabriel's beliefs. "I know, I know, every Mer is precious, but how did I get so damned lucky that you were the one to find me? And take such good care of me? Surely you have duties and a lot more important things to do!"

Finding you was … was meant, Casillus said as he ran his fingers through the warm water, which had Gabriel licking his lips. He felt so parched again.

"Meant?" Gabriel's stomach fluttered.

I was called and you were there. This is meant.

Gabriel wanted to ask more about this call, but there was still a sense that Casillus was holding something back. Gabriel didn't think he was holding something bad back, but rather something Casillus did not want to discuss at that moment. In any event, it was a strange cautiousness for the normally open Mer.

Casillus added, *House Liseas is the most important House after Nerion. House Nerion and House Liseas have a long history of friendship.*

"Well, that's cool, but I'm not exactly an important person in House Liseas. Not important enough for the prince of all Mer to be my personal guide into Mer-dom," Gabriel pointed out. He realized he had acknowledged that he was some part of Mer society right there. It felt both right and strange.

On the contrary, Aemrys is the head of House Liseas. You are quite important, Casillus pointed out.

Gabriel shook his head. "Clearly, I have a lot to learn."

And I have the time and desire to teach you. Come into the water, Gabriel. Casillus extended one hand towards him, and Gabriel found he didn't want to resist the water's—*or Casillus'*—pull any longer.

"All right. You win. I will 'shed' my clothes." Gabriel pulled off his shirt without much thought and tossed it into the corner, but then his hands went to his shorts. His eyes snapped up and met Casillus' gaze at that moment. The Mer was looking at him rather avidly. There was no hiding his interest.

What is wrong, Gabriel? Why do you hesitate?

"I just … nothing." It wasn't nothing. It was shyness. It was fear that the Mer would not like what he saw. But Gabriel undid the button on his shorts. He grasped the waistband and his underwear, and in one fluid motion he pushed both down to his ankles. Then he stepped out of his clothes. He was naked but for the kalish around his neck. It felt cool against his bare skin. When he straightened up, he immediately looked at the Mer's face again to see his reaction. Casillus was studying his body. The Mer's eyes slid up and down Gabriel's form. Gabriel forced his hands to remain at his sides and his limbs to not tighten up. "Well? What do you think? Am I Mer material?"

The question was meant to be half joking, but Gabriel couldn't help but compare his own physique to Casillus'. He had never had any concerns about how he looked, but Casillus was on a whole other level of beauty that left him feeling insecure about his own attractiveness.

You are … so lovely, Casillus suddenly breathed out after he had completed his inspection.

"Oh, good, I was worried there for a moment." Gabriel let out a self-conscious laugh.

You will bring great pride to House Liseas for your incredible mind and healthy form, Casillus continued in a serious vein. *Aemrys' joy at finding you may actually eclipse his grief.*

"He still mourns Tabatha?" Gabriel couldn't imagine mourning someone for a hundred years, but maybe that showed more about his own shallowness than the impossibility of it.

Casillus nodded. *He mourns what could have been.*

"What about his son? Didn't he come and visit him?" Gabriel asked.

His child could not take to the water, but the child never left this house by the sea. Aemrys came and saw him often. On the day of his son's death, Aemrys helped the old man his son had become into the waves and held him as he passed, Casillus said.

Gabriel was stunned into silence for a moment. The image was both beautiful and incredibly sad. "His son didn't live forever because he didn't have enough of the Mer gene?"

Yes, he could not take to the water so the other gifts of the Mers were lost as well, Casillus explained.

At that moment, Gabriel realized that the bath was nearly overflowing. He dove for the faucet's handles and cranked both into the off position. The small drain set into the side of the tub had been sipping down the water, but couldn't keep up with the flow. Now that the deluge from the faucet was gone, it started to lower the water to a manageable level. Gabriel gave a laugh as he turned on his knees towards Casillus.

"That was close. I think flooding the bathroom would definitely cause my grandmother to wake up," Gabriel said.

Yes, and my presence would require some explanation.

"Oh, yeah, I can only imagine how I would explain a merman in my grandmother's bathtub," Gabriel agreed.

His eyes met and caught the Mer's once more. *Love always shows up first in the eyes.* His mother's phrase repeated in his mind as he became lost once more in Casillus' blue-green gaze.

Will you get in now? The water level is low enough that it will not overflow, the Mer said. There was a sensual tint to his voice.

Gabriel's gaze dropped down to the water. Seeing Casillus' almost naked body with his legs invitingly spread was almost too much for him. He stood up on numb legs and found himself stepping into the tub without further thought or conversation. He sank down into the hot water. He let out a sigh as the water covered him. He pushed his legs out towards the faucet. The soft, silky slide of Casillus' inner thighs against his legs was heavenly.

Casillus urged Gabriel to lay back against his chest. Gabriel slowly did so. He felt the long length of Casillus' cock against his ass and lower spine. He shivered in pleasure. Casillus was half erect. The Mer brought his hands up and began to gently pour water over Gabriel's pectoral muscles. Almost immediately Gabriel felt the itching in his sides and he tensed up in alarm.

Gabriel? What is it?

It's happening again! My sides—the gills! They're—they're coming out! Gabriel found himself naturally falling into mindspeak as panic settled in. It allowed him to hold onto Casillus mentally and physically. He tried to sit up but the Mer held him still.

Be calm, Gabriel. Let it happen, Casillus soothed.

Gabriel was tense as a bow, but Casillus continued to stroke his chest and hair, urging him to lay back again. The itching in his sides increased. His heart hammered. Would it happen again? Would the gills appear? If they did there was no more hiding from the fact that he was a Mer. He felt the almost familiar sensation of his skin *unzipping* and then his difficulty breathing was suddenly just *gone.* Gabriel went still as a statue. He could feel the gills moving along his sides. Feel them fluttering.

Good, Gabriel. You did it, Casillus said.

I did ... what?

Look down, Casillus urged.

Gabriel shuddered, but he slowly let his gaze slide down to his sides. The gills were there. Just like Casillus'. A Mer's body looked back at him. He was a Mer.

Gabriel found himself letting out a choked sob. He tried to cover his mouth, to keep the sound in, but Casillus was turning him so that Gabriel's head was tucked between his chin and chest. Gabriel's hands clutched at him.

I'm a Mer! Casillus, I'm a Mer!

Casillus pressed a gentle kiss against his right temple. *Yes, Gabriel, you are.*

Chapter 7

LOST AND FOUND

abriel wasn't sure how long he spent clutching Casillus. The Mer smoothed his webbed hands down Gabriel's back. His heart rate slowed and evened out as the stroking continued. Gabriel didn't have webbing between his fingers yet, but the gills were definitely there. It almost tickled when the flaps of skin fluttered as he breathed. He wanted to look at them again, but that would mean breaking free of Casillus' embrace and he didn't want to do that yet.

You have calmed now. The Mer's voice was soft like the rush of the waves.

I'm too tired to be upset. Calm takes less energy, Gabriel admitted with a laugh. He rested his cheek against the Mer's broad shoulder and rubbed it surreptitiously against the Mer's slick skin. It felt so right to be in Casillus' arms. He knew he should get up and stop hugging the Mer, but he didn't want to. He never wanted to get up. *I was fighting the change so hard. Now that I'm just letting it happen, there's nothing left to fight anymore, I guess. I can finally relax.*

I can tell. You are quite relaxed in my arms, Casillus chuckled. He stroked Gabriel's back again, which nearly made the young man purr.

It's all true. You. Me. Mermen and mermaids. God, if anyone knew ... He thought of Johnson Tims' gray eyes alighting with interest if he discovered Mers existed. He shivered. Even after just one meeting, Gabriel knew that a man like Johnson Tims would never be content just knowing that Mers existed. He wouldn't be satisfied until he had seen the Mers and their city himself. And maybe even that wouldn't be enough.

There was—perhaps, is—a rule that only immediate family can know about the ones who transition, Casillus said. *It has been so long since one of our half-human offspring transitioned that it is unclear to me if the rules still apply.*

Well, whether they apply or not, my grandmother and Corey ARE my family so I guess it should be okay either way, Gabriel said. Corey might not be his blood brother, but no one could be closer to him than his best friend.

You feel you can trust them. That is important. Grace ... Grace has Mer blood, too, Casillus said.

But not enough. Like my father and mother, she doesn't have enough, Gabriel said, and a tremor ran through him. He would have to leave her. She couldn't come into the water with him.

She will always have a connection to you and to the Mer. When the time comes for her to pass on—

No, Casillus, please, don't talk about that. I don't want to think of her dying. He shut his eyes tightly. *She and Corey will be so upset about losing me. I don't want to think about losing them permanently.*

They will not lose you, Gabriel. Yes, you will go into the sea,

75

but you will not be lost, Casillus said.

They won't see it that way, Gabriel struggled to explain. *There won't be an apartment with Corey next year. No summer of sifting through the Braven family history. No Fourth of July fireworks while Corey and I drink too much beer. No more of Grandma's pies. There won't be another Christmas where we get sick on eggnog and end up opening gifts too early.* Gabriel stopped listing things off. It was too painful. It felt like he was going to choke on everything he was going to lose.

You are losing many things. I grieve with you over them, Casillus said.

Those aren't just words, are they? I feel your pain for me. Gabriel's breathing hitched. Trying to imagine what he was losing was just too much, yet feeling Casillus *inside* of him was equally as moving in an entirely different way.

Yes, Gabriel, I am with you. I will always be with you. Know now that for as much as you are losing, you are gaining so many things as well, Casillus said. Gabriel could feel the Mer's lips move against his temple even though he did not use his mouth to speak. Was it a kiss? An accidental touch? *I know you cannot see it yet, but there is so much happiness awaiting you.*

I actually can sort of believe that. If you are any indication of what I have to look forward to, Gabriel said, feeling bold and his grief dampening somewhat, *Then I have nothing to fear. But ...*

But no one and nothing can replace Corey and Grace, Casillus completed Gabriel's thought.

You understand. It seems so unfair to lose them. I want to share all this with them, but I can't.

Love the moment, Gabriel. Do not waste it on fears for the future, Casillus said.

Gabriel's eyebrows rose. *You live forever and you believe that?*

It is because I live forever that I believe that, Casillus said. *Because I know that there is nothing like the present.*

76

Seize the day, right?

Seize the moment. Casillus' hand lingered at the swell of Gabriel's buttocks, and a different type of tension suddenly crept into them both.

Gabriel became hyper aware of his own cock pressed tightly against Casillus' taut stomach. The Mer's cock was pushed against Gabriel's left thigh. Heat flooded his belly. He knew that his cock would start to harden and twitch any moment. He should get up. He *needed* to get up before he embarrassed himself and Casillus with his arousal.

You would not embarrass me by becoming aroused. Casillus' voice was a rumble in his mind.

You—you heard that thought? Of course you did. No secrets between Mer. Gabriel flushed and hid his face against Casillus' chest even though he should have been leaping away from the Mer, not drawing nearer to him.

Only because you wanted me to know. And I am so glad you did. Casillus' hand that had been resting on Gabriel's back lowered and caressed along the length of Gabriel's crevice.

You're glad? You—you want me, too? Gabriel stilled even as his mind melted from that intimate caress. Had he read Casillus right? Was he understanding what the Mer was saying? He suddenly wished he could heard the Mer's thoughts and feelings as clearly as Casillus could hear his. Perhaps after the transition he would, but for now the Mer's feelings were opaque to him.

Casillus' lips pressed against Gabriel's right temple. They lingered there. This time it was a kiss. An unmistakable kiss. *How could I not want you? You have no idea how you call to me.*

Gabriel pulled back from Casillus' chest so that he could see the Mer's face. Casillus' blue-green eyes looked back into his. The Mer's naturally large pupils were even larger than usual. Gabriel ran one hand along his jaw. Casillus' eyelids fell half closed as Gabriel caressed him. The length of his cock hardened against Gabriel's thigh. Gabriel's own cock throbbed in response.

You mentioned a call before. Is this the same thing? Gabriel asked.

No, that was something I was doing for our people, Casillus said and blinked. He wouldn't quite meet Gabriel's gaze then. *This is just for me.*

I'm just for you? A smile slowly grew on Gabriel's face.

Will you allow that, Gabriel? Casillus looked at him through hooded eyes. *Will you allow me to have you?*

Gabriel's heart thrilled inside of him. *I think I would allow almost anything you wanted.*

Desire rippled across their bond. Casillus' pupils grew even larger, but then Gabriel felt him pull back and ask, *But are you ready for this? You are still weak and in the midst of the transition—*

Not that weak. Heat flooded Gabriel's body once more. His cock did twitch this time and he eagerly pushed against the Mer. The thought of sex with Casillus suddenly had him feeling strong and capable. He surged up in the water and leaned into the Mer as if to say, "See, I'm fine!"

Casillus smiled as he stared deeply into Gabriel's eyes. He was clearly reading Gabriel's desire, but also, Gabriel was almost certain that the Mer was seeing the weakness that he wanted to hide, too. *We will compromise, then.*

A compromise? Gabriel's eyebrows rose.

Instead of answering, Casillus threaded the fingers of his right hand through Gabriel's hair and drew their mouths together. Their first kiss was like a revelation. It wasn't just the physical sensation of soft, plush lips opening under his or the sweet tangle of their tongues, but the heightened mental connection.

It was like their nervous systems were one. Gabriel could feel the coolness of the tub behind Casillus' back, the warm slosh of water around the Mer's limbs, and the pulse of his own cock against Casillus' belly from the Mer's perspective. He felt Casillus' arousal burning brighter and brighter. His own arousal roared even higher in response, his cock quivering like an eager dog on a leash. His balls felt so hot and tight that he thought they might burst, but the arousal was nothing compared to the sense of connection. That connection crashed over Gabriel, overwhelmed him, and his strength flowed away.

Gabriel? Casillus asked, pulling back.

It was ... was incredible, but ...

Too much. It was too much, the Mer realized, and Gabriel nodded. He realized that Casillus sounded rather breathless and dazed himself, as if what they had experienced wasn't normal for him either. *I have you. Relax. Relax, Gabriel. Let me hold you up.*

Despite breaking off the kiss the connection still snapped between them like a live electrical wire, but it wasn't as disorienting. Gabriel trembled, but forced himself to let Casillus bear his weight in the water. He suddenly noticed the fine tremors that were running through Casillus as well. Had the Mer been overwhelmed by the connection, too?

Was that as good for you as it was for me? Gabriel let out a weak laugh.

A shiver ran through Casillus before he answered, *It was ... like nothing else. I—I did not know it could happen, but then House Liseas has produced one before you. Still, never has a transitioned human become one. Yet our need sent me out ... and I found you.*

Casillus' thoughts and words were jumbled and perplexing. What couldn't a transitioned human become? What had House Liseas produced before? What had Casillus been looking for? But Gabriel stopped himself from asking all of those questions. He could feel the Mer's confusion and shock coursing over their bond. The Mer seemed so overwhelmed and unsure that Gabriel didn't want to cause more of those emotions by pressing right at that moment. So instead, he chose what he hoped would be a "light" question.

So it isn't always like this between Mer? Surprising jealousy squirmed inside of Gabriel. He did not want to believe that Casillus had had this with someone else. It felt so *special*. It felt so *unique*.

No, no, nothing like that. The mental connection is there, but ... Casillus' head tilted to the side, eyes filled with confusion as he sorted through Gabriel's experiences, but then his gaze cleared. *Ah, I see. When humans mate there is no mind to mind connection. It is only body to body.*

Mate? Uh, yeah, right, mate. Gabriel colored. That word seemed so much sexier than "make out" or "have sex". It also sounded more adult or something. *Humans don't share minds, thoughts, feelings ... nothing like what just happened between us.* The snapping of the connection caused him to add, *What continues to happen between us. I guess there's no such thing as meaningless sex for Mers, is there, especially with something like this between them.*

Why would anyone want it to be meaningless? Casillus looked almost appalled at the thought.

Needing to feel some connection, even physical, is a powerful motive. Emotional connections can be messy. They can be painful, Gabriel confessed uncomfortably.

But such a coupling without any emotional connection would feel dead inside, wouldn't it? Casillus asked. His eyes filled with pain as he considered it.

Sometimes, perhaps, but when it's all you have, when it's all you believe you'll ever have ... you think it's enough. At the time, anyways. Gabriel was speaking from personal experience. *Humans don't even know about the possibility of something like this between people. Mer have a leg up on that, I guess.*

What we experienced today is ... rare, so very rare, even among the Mer, Casillus said carefully.

Gabriel blinked. That was how he had viewed his parents' relationship—so very rare. *It is?*

Casillus touched Gabriel's cheek. *Yes, what we experienced is extraordinary.*

It felt extraordinary to me, but I wasn't sure if it was just my ignorance of what being Mer means. Gabriel gave Casillus a smile.

The connection—*no, bond*—was buzzing pleasantly through him wherever they physically touched.

Casillus stared at him, unblinking, for long moments, saying nothing. Despite there being a bone between them, Gabriel couldn't touch the Mer's mind at all in that moment. He wondered desperately what was going on in Casillus' brain, but then the Mer blinked. He had come to some decision, though Gabriel had no idea what he had been deciding about. He said simply, *It is very special.*

Gabriel knew that there was more to it than that. Casillus was holding back something. At first, Gabriel wanted to drag it out of the Mer. *But the only reason Casillus wouldn't tell me something is because he believes I'm not ready to know. Do I trust him to determine that?* One look into those blue-green eyes had Gabriel feeling sure that he did trust Casillus enough to let it go for now.

The Mer suddenly leaned in and pressed his lips against Gabriel's again. This time Gabriel was almost prepared for the onslaught of the connection. Their closeness sizzled across his and Casillus' skin. There was no difference between their bodies now. A sense of oneness filled Gabriel again. He struggled to get up on his knees between Casillus' powerful thighs so that he could more easily kiss and stroke that beautiful body and face. Weakness weighed down his limbs, but he fought it. Suddenly Casillus' strength surged inside of him, helping him move easily.

We should stop, Gabriel, Casillus warned. *I can feel how the transition is weakening you. You need to rest.*

I can't stop. I don't want to stop. And you don't either. Gabriel could read that clearly in the Mer's swirling emotions.

But I don't want to hurt you more than anything else I feel, Casillus insisted.

It'll be all right. Just give me this, Casillus. Please. Gabriel's mind voice was just a murmur as they continued to kiss. It was hard to form coherent sentences as the electricity sparked between them wildly.

What do you want? What do you need? Casillus moaned into

the kiss.

For us to ... Gabriel couldn't form the words. Instead he sent an image of the two of them with their heads thrown back, arms around one another and cum streaming from their bodies. *Can we have that? I want that so badly.*

Gabriel was shocked by the need in him. The thought of sharing this with Casillus seemed so right. The emptiness that he had never wanted to admit was inside of him might actually be ... quenched, in some way. It was already retreating the longer they kissed. Almost.

You can have it, Gabriel. I give myself to you, the Mer whispered. The words seemed to flow into Gabriel's blood like a drug, and he found he couldn't resist them even if he had wanted to.

Gabriel moved to straddle Casillus' lap. Their cocks bobbed in the water between them. Casillus' organ was long and thick. The tip was huge and rose colored. There was a gauzy haze of precum in the water surrounding it. Gabriel licked his lips. He could almost taste the Mer's semen on his tongue. Casillus clasped both their cocks in one of his large hands.

The feeling of his cock being touched by Casillus had Gabriel nearly levitating out of the water. The Mer began stroking both their cocks from root to tip. The pressure was just right. Not too hard or soft, but *firm* and *commanding*. As their lips met again and again Gabriel thrust forward against the Mer, his movement causing his cock to slide upwards in Casillus' grip. He let out a whine. Casillus' free hand wound around Gabriel's back and cupped his ass. His fingers played along the crack. Gabriel's hips rose and fell eagerly. The water in the tub sloshed over the sides, but neither of them cared. Their bodies sparked with their combined energy.

Casillus' thumb slid over the head of Gabriel's penis, spreading open his slit. Hot precum gushed out. Gabriel's hands raked down Casillus' front. He found the Mer's nipples and tweaked them. Casillus jerked in pleasure and the bond went purple with desire. Every thought and feeling between them was blood red and then brilliant sea blue, melding together as their hips moved in unison.

Casillus' fingers slipped between Gabriel's ass cheeks. He slowly drew them up towards the tight pink pucker of Gabriel's anus. Gabriel let out a gasp into one of their kisses. Being touched *there*, where he was so vulnerable and so very needy, made him feel like he was touching a powerline. Every cell inside of him tingled. Casillus hesitated, reading his gasp as pain, his fingers millimeters from that tender opening. There was a little pain. The twin arousals he was experiencing through their bond were so strong, so overwhelming to his mind that he fully expected to pass out from it, but at the same time, he wanted that touch more than anything.

Touch me! Touch me, please! Gabriel commanded and begged at the same time.

Casillus' fingers brushed over the surface of his anus. Gabriel dug his fingers into Casillus' shoulders as black spots appeared before his eyes. He was seeing and feeling everything from both Casillus' perspective and his own. It was like being two people at once.

Touch me, touch me, touch me, Gabriel repeated over and over again.

Casillus' mouth fastened onto Gabriel's, his tongue sliding deeply inside just as he gently pushed two fingers inside of Gabriel's ass. Gabriel screamed in pleasure into Casillus' mouth. Thankfully, the seal of the Mer's lips kept the sound from escaping and the whole house from hearing. He clenched the muscles in his anus down on those beautiful fingers, wanting to keep them inside of him as both their arousals crested at the same time. It felt like being on top of a wave that was going to crash onto a sandy beach. The pleasure was almost unbearably painful as their balls drew tight to their bodies and both their cocks grew so hard it felt like they would explode.

Just as semen began to pour from their cocks, spurting out onto their bellies, Casillus slid his fingers deeper inside Gabriel's ass and rubbed his prostate firmly. Gabriel arched back. His mouth opened in a wordless cry as his body emptied itself of every ounce of sperm.

Gabriel collapsed forward onto Casillus. Half of the bath water had sloshed out onto the floor, but Gabriel just couldn't care even though it left his gills only partially covered by the water. His body was just too blasted by his orgasm to worry about breathing after that. The Mer's arms wound around him, holding him tightly against his chest. He knew that Casillus was nearly as blown away as he was.

Gabriel, oh, my Gabriel, Casillus said, and other tender, nonsensical things flowed over their bond that had Gabriel's lips twitching into a smile even as the black spots that had danced before his eyes earlier grew larger and larger until he realized that it was unconsciousness pulling him down.

But at the last moment before blackness hit he thought he saw something over their bond, something in Casillus' mind. Something the Mer *eagerly* wanted to happen, something Casillus believed *would* happen because Gabriel was transitioning. This something was miles high with tentacles. It was streaming out of the deep and swimming towards shore.

Towards them.

Gabriel told himself it was just a remnant of his own dream, because such a horrible creature could have nothing to do with the beautiful Mers.

Chapter 8

SEEN

Smuggling a merman out of the house before the first light of dawn was far more difficult than Gabriel thought it would be. His grandmother was a notoriously early riser so he had meant to stay awake and lead Casillus to the sea around 3:00 a.m. But he had fallen asleep. Deeply asleep. Casillus hadn't had the heart to wake him either. Now it was almost 6:00 a.m. and the sun was already rising, and Gabriel was sure that he heard his grandmother moving around in her room.

Grace is stirring. I can almost hear her thoughts, Casillus said. Gabriel turned to look over at the Mer. Casillus' head was tilted to the side. His blue-green eyes were luminous as he concentrated on hearing her thoughts. *Even after so many years, House Liseas' blood runs strongly through her veins.*

Gabriel barely refrained from responding, *Not strongly*

enough. Instead, he said, *I hope I'll be able to hear her some day.*

Casillus cupped his face before leaning in and kissing him deeply. *You will. You will hear all the Mer and you will never be alone.*

You know that still freaks me out a little bit, right? Gabriel smiled as they rested their foreheads together. *Being connected to you is one thing, but to others? To people I don't know who don't know me? I'm not certain about that.*

Casillus' eyes flickered away from his for a moment, and once again he felt shut out of the Mer's thoughts. *You may find that connections are ... in your nature.*

Mers weren't supposed to have secrets, yet it seemed that Casillus was keeping a few from him at this moment. He told himself that Casillus must have his reasons and that the Mer would reveal all in time.

Maybe you're right, Gabriel said. *I'd better get some clothes on so that we can get you back to the sea.*

Casillus nodded. *I wish you were going with me, Gabriel, but I know that you are not ready yet.*

Gabriel paused in pulling on his shorts. If Casillus was right, he had three days left on land at most. His mouth went dry. He responded slowly, *You're right. I'm not ready, though ... I don't want to be away from you either.*

I will never leave you, remember? Casillus put a finger under Gabriel's chin and tipped it up so that they were eye to eye.

Gabriel found himself getting lost in that gaze. Everything became unimportant in comparison to Casillus. Everything except the clock ticking down. His chest went tight again, and this time his difficulty breathing didn't come from a physical cause but a mental one. Three days. He only had three days. Three days to say goodbye. Three days to leave everything and everyone he knew and loved.

I need ... more time to say goodbye to my grandmother and Corey. I have to arrange an explanation about my disappearance.

And then—

Casillus touched Gabriel's temples and shook his head gently. *Forgive me, I did not mean to cause you pain or panic with that wish. I know you need time. I would not take it away from you.*

Gabriel's shoulders slumped and he leaned against Casillus' bigger form. *I know you wouldn't. It's just ... three days. That's all I have left. If I'm lucky. It just hit me for a second. How can I go into the sea when it still ... still frightens me?*

Casillus was quiet for a moment. *Today, after you go to the site, will you come to me?*

Of course ... oh, you mean go into the water with you? Gabriel stiffened.

For a swim. We won't leave the shallows. You'll be able to stand, Casillus assured him. *It would be a first step.*

A vision of the two of them splashing in the surf under the warm summer sun flashed through his mind. It would be playful. It would be safe. It would be far from what he had experienced with his parents.

A first step? Yeah, maybe—maybe that would be good.

I am pleased, Casillus said, and over their bond his pleasure was spiced with desire.

Another vision flashed through his mind then: kissing in the surf with their limbs tangled together as their tongues slid against one another. He could almost taste the salt on his tongue.

I want that, Gabriel said.

He didn't have to tell Casillus what he meant. He knew he had shared that image with the Mer. Casillus leaned down and kissed him. Gabriel's heart beat faster. His cock stirred again.

I'm missing you already. Gabriel's mind voice was a whisper as the kiss ended.

Soon we will never be parted, Casillus pointed out, but Gabriel felt the Mer's reluctance to physically move away from him.

Gabriel was the one to pull back from the Mer. He thought he heard his grandmother's voice. He hastily reached for his shirt, but it was soaked. With a grimace, he dropped it back on the floor. The gills at his sides were settling down now, but the wet shirt would just reactivate them. He worried, too, that the gills would show through the clingy material even if he did put it on, and it would take too long to grab a fresh shirt from his room. He was certain that his grandmother would emerge from her room at any second. They had to go.

Casillus confirmed that when his head tilted to the side again and he said, *Your grandmother is getting up from her bed. She is preparing to put on her dressing gown and go downstairs. I must leave.*

Gabriel shut off the bathroom light before he opened the door. He stuck his head out. His grandmother's door was still closed. Corey's snores were still drifting down the hall in soft wheezes. Gabriel motioned for Casillus to follow him out into the hall.

Padding down the hallway and stairs was like running an obstacle course of creaking floorboards and groaning banisters. No matter where they stepped or touched, it made a sound. After a very loud crack, Gabriel said, *Forget stealth. Let's do speed.*

Gabriel and Casillus hustled down the stairs, through the hall to the kitchen and then out the back door to the porch. Gabriel didn't take a breath until they were both standing on the sand. The sun's rays were just starting to kiss the horizon. Gabriel spun around towards the Mer.

We made it! Gabriel grinned.

Casillus' arms wound around his waist and he pulled Gabriel against him. *I am not in the water yet.*

No, not yet. Gabriel's heart clenched. *I know we'll still be connected, but it's going to be so hard seeing you go back into the water while I remain behind.*

You will see me this afternoon. It will not be so long. The Mer looked at him so fondly that Gabriel's heartbeat sped up.

Right. Swimming together today, Gabriel said.

The Mer nodded. Another soft kiss and he pulled away. They both looked out at the sea. The horizon was glowing, kissed by the rising sun. The waves were a deep blue with creamy white tops. For a moment, Gabriel felt that sensation again, that feeling that something amazing was out there, waiting for him. With Casillus at his side, Gabriel could almost imagine going out to meet it.

I must go now, Gabriel, Casillus' voice interrupted his thoughts. *Grace is about to walk into the kitchen. She will be able to see me through the window.*

You have to go. Yet Gabriel's hands clung to the Mer.

Yes, Casillus whispered. He stroked Gabriel's cheek and then took a step back. *I am always with you. I will never leave you.*

I believe you. Gabriel found himself giving Casillus a wobbly smile as he let go of the Mer physically. It actually hurt to do it, but he stopped himself from clutching Casillus back to him no matter how much he wanted to. *Go on. Before she sees you.*

Casillus stared at Gabriel as if memorizing his face before he turned and dashed into the water. Gabriel watched that beautiful body dive into the dark blue waves. After a moment, Casillus' head popped up through the surface for one last look back at him.

I will never leave you, Casillus said.

Gabriel smiled even as Casillus' head disappeared beneath the waves once more. He was about to ask the Mer how the water was, or even look through Casillus' eyes at the fish that were undoubtedly darting away, but there was a sound from behind him.

Gabriel whipped around. He was not comforted by what he saw. Instead, his heart began to race and his chest tightened painfully again. Johnson Tims was standing in the doorway of the house. The sound Gabriel had heard was the screech of the screen door opening, but the real question was how long had Johnson been standing *in* the doorway? How much had he seen?

The Story Continues in Book 3!

The

Merman

BOOK 3 – CALLER

~A PREVIEW~

Chapter 1

FOOTSTEPS IN THE SAND

abriel Braven met Johnson Tims' gray gaze and wondered if the older man had seen the Mer Prince Casillus Nerion dive beneath the ocean's surface. Because if Johnson had, things were about to get very interesting.

"Johnson! I—I didn't hear you come—come out," Gabriel said lamely, gesturing to the porch where the man stood. "How long have you been standing there?"

Watching me? Watching Casillus? Spying on us?

Johnson Tims was a former military man-turned-professor at the mysterious and secretive Miskatonic University and, evidently, also Gabriel's grandmother's boyfriend. After all, why would the man be in a robe at 6:00 a.m. on Grace's porch unless he had spent the night? But standing there in the morning light, Johnson didn't look like a man blinded by love. Instead, his bright, inquisitive gaze was completely clear. Too clear.

What am I thinking? That he spent the night with my grandmother to be near me? That he's seducing her so that he can find out if Mer blood still runs strong in Braven veins? That's crazy.

Then again, Gabriel had thought believing mermen were real was crazy, too. However, not only were mermen real, he was transforming into one of them.

Johnson walked down the steps and onto the beach that spread out from the back of his grandmother's cottage in a fan of gold. The black robe he wore strained over the bulging muscles in his arms. The end of it hung to just above his knees. Gabriel guessed it wasn't Johnson's own robe by how tight it was and how little it covered. It didn't look like one of his grandmother's either, so that left it being his grandfather's, a man whom Gabriel had never met as he had died before Gabriel was born.

Wearing a dead man's clothes? That's sort of creepy. But it's certainly better than seeing him naked.

"I'm surprised to see you up and looking so … *refreshed,* Gabriel," Johnson said as he stopped alongside him. "You seemed so ill at dinner last night."

And I thought you went home after that dinner, but evidently not. We're both full of surprises.

He had spent the night in the bathtub in Casillus' arms with water surrounding them both. That had relieved some of the weakness that now plagued Gabriel as his body transformed from human to merman. He resisted the urge to touch his sides and assure himself that his gills, which appeared when he got wet, had disappeared. If faint traces of them still remained it would only draw Johnson's attention to them, so he kept his hands down.

In some ways, the fact that Gabriel was becoming a merman was the most ridiculous thing that could ever happen to him. He had been afraid of the sea since he was a child. His fear had started after his parents had drowned in a terrible storm on the ocean. Seemingly miraculously, Gabriel had survived the sinking of their boat by two rogue waves, but his love of the ocean had died that day along with his parents. After their deaths, Gabriel had feared and loathed the water as much as he had formerly loved it. And then, just yesterday, Gabriel had nearly drowned *again*. This time, he had been rescued by Casillus Nerion, a prince of the Mers. Casillus had told Gabriel the truth about why he had survived drowning twice. Gabriel was a Mer, too.

Casillus explained that Gabriel's ancestors on both sides must have had Mer blood, and once combined in him, there was enough merman DNA that he was transitioning into a Mer. The change normally took place much earlier in life, but Gabriel's avoidance of the sea had delayed the transition.

Gabriel hadn't believed Casillus at first. After all, mermen did *not* exist. Like unicorns and Santa Claus, they weren't real. But Gabriel had ultimately had to accept the truth as his breathing became more and more labored out of the water and gills started appearing on his sides whenever he got wet. The physical transformation had pretty much sealed the deal as far as proof went. He was not human. Then Casillus had told him one more thing. Mers lived forever, but Gabriel would die unless he entered the water. He only had three days left on land before he had to go into the sea and transition fully into a Mer. Three days to say goodbye to all he loved and go into the ocean he still feared.

The existence of Mers and his transition into one of them had to be kept secret from humans. Only his grandmother and his best friend Corey Rudman could ever know. Gabriel hadn't had a chance to tell them yet, but Johnson, with his cold eyes and military mindset, seemed to have guessed something. At least, he *suspected* something.

What does he suspect? What does he know?

"Yeah, well, a good night's sleep helped," Gabriel said finally.

Johnson's slate gray gaze, which had been sweeping the water looking for something—*or someone*—turned towards him. "I wouldn't have thought sleeping in a bathtub would be that restful."

"How did you know I slept there?" Gabriel tensed. "I mean, yeah, I did—did take a bath last night and I fell asleep in the tub, but how do you know that?"

"I thought I heard the bath running last night. It woke me up, and then I heard your voice. You must have been talking to yourself." Johnson's gaze was opaque.

Talking to myself? Oh, shit, that was when I was INSISTING to Casillus that it was too intimate to speak through our bond. Why was I so stupid?

"Yeah, I do that sometimes. Talk to myself out loud about … about things," Gabriel said.

Gabriel immediately shut down his mental bond with Casillus. This bond allowed them to speak to one another telepathically. He felt as though shutting it down would keep the Mer safer from Johnson somehow.

"You had a lot to talk out, then," Johnson said.

"And you, ah, listened?" Gabriel's mouth went dry. What had he said out loud? How much of it could Johnson make out?

Johnson dug his toes into the soft, warm sand. "You mustn't worry. I didn't clearly hear what you said. Just the cadence of your voice rising and falling."

"Oh, I—I see."

And he heard all of this from my grandmother's bed? For a moment, Gabriel envisioned Johnson and Grace's bodies entwined. *Gah! I have to put that image out of my mind. Then again, I was doing things with Casillus that would curl their hair and we were in the tub just down the hall, so I guess we're even.*

Johnson continued on, "By the *length* of your conversation, I could tell that you were quite concerned about something. Is it something I could help you with?"

Help me? Gabriel's gaze slid to the sea. It was beautiful and terrifying, and he had no idea how he was ever going to live in it for eternity. He wished he could talk to Casillus at that moment, but the silence was better. He was protecting the Mer.

Johnson touched Gabriel's shoulder. "I can tell you're troubled. You don't have to bear this burden alone."

For one wild moment, Gabriel considered telling him. Without Casillus there to take away his doubts and fears he suddenly felt like he would explode. Johnson's expression was almost gentle and definitely concerned. The urge to confess was so strong that Gabriel actually opened his mouth to speak, but then he saw the coldness lurking behind Johnson's eyes. His mouth snapped shut. Revealing any of this to Johnson would be crazy. His confession would be to Corey and his grandmother, not to this ex-military man.

The only reason I even considered telling him is because I've cut myself off from Casillus, Gabriel realized with a start. *I'm alone again and I'm not thinking straight.*

Shaking himself, Gabriel said, "No, it's nothing you can help me with. It's something that I've got to deal with on my own."

On my own ... no, I'm not on my own. Casillus is with me. He's out there. Watching. Waiting. Caring for me. And Corey and my grandmother are here for me as well. I'm not alone. Repeating that to himself helped calm down his frantic thoughts.

"But on your own, you fell asleep in a tub full of water," Johnson pointed out.

"I—"

"You need to be more careful, Gabriel. You could *drown* doing something like that," Johnson said too casually.

Gabriel found himself stepping back. He hadn't meant to react to Johnson's words, but he couldn't help it. "Y—yeah, but I'm fine. Clearly, I didn't—I didn't *drown*."

Terror had him thinking, *He knows!*

But what did, or could, Johnson know? That Mers existed?

His mind offered, *He saw Casillus dive into the sea!*

But then his mind then offered, *He can't know Mers are real even if he did see Casillus. Casillus looks just like a normal man. Albeit, an extremely beautiful, nearly naked man who disappeared under the waves and never surfaced for air ...*

Gabriel mentally shook himself. *He can't know! He knows nothing!*

"You didn't drown *this time*," Johnson corrected quietly, but then he gave Gabriel a stern look. "And not the time with your parents either. One would almost say that the water loves you. That or you're exceptionally lucky."

"The sea took my parents! That's not *love!*" Gabriel snapped.

"Forgive me, Gabriel," he said. "I shouldn't have said it the way I did."

"You shouldn't have said it at all!" Gabriel shouted. His throat felt raw.

"It's just ... so *strange* how you survived that day when your parents did not. When *no one* should have. You were *miles* away from land. The storm was the most powerful in a *century*. I can't even imagine what the ocean must have been like. Waves as tall as buildings bearing down on you. Rain like knives hitting your skin. Yet you managed to *swim* to shore although you were just a little boy," Johnson said, and as he spoke, Gabriel remembered.

But Gabriel didn't remember the waves or rain. He remembered looking up and seeing the storm raging far, far, far above him. He was safe. The lightning that streaked the sky illuminated the water around him ... the water ... he was underwater ... being carried by tentacles like he was the most precious of treasures ...

Gabriel blinked and the memory disappeared. His gaze jerked to the sea. He expected to see the sky turning black and the waves rising and rising and rising. But the sky was clear and the sea was almost flat. It was a calm day. A beautiful day. Sweat coated his forehead and upper lip.

That wasn't real. That couldn't be real. Casillus, I need you. But he did not reach for the Mer. He had to keep it together and keep Casillus safe.

"Do you ever wonder about why you survived?" Johnson asked. It was more than asking, it was probing.

Gabriel's back straightened. The urge to flee flowed over him. *But where would I go? And what would he think? If he has suspicions about me, running would clearly confirm them. I have to keep calm.*

Gabriel took in a deep breath and turned back to Johnson before he said, "I've been thinking about it a lot since I've been back here." He crossed his arms over his chest and looked out at the water once more. Casillus was out there. The sea was not as frightening as it had been now that he knew the Mer was right there. Nearly touchable. Casillus would let nothing happen to him. "Coming back here is bringing up a lot of memories. Not all of them are good."

"The day of the storm being one of those bad memories, I'm sure," Johnson said.

"Y—yeah, the worst." Gabriel blinked back sudden tears. The image of his mother and father being dragged down by the boat as it sank flashed through his mind. He had dreamt of the sinking just last night. The dream had been so vivid, so real, that his sadness at their deaths was now almost as fresh to him as if they had just happened.

"Your grandmother said that you *directed* where you and your parents sailed that day," Johnson said.

Gabriel stiffened once more, and then his head snapped towards Johnson in surprise. "She *told* you that?"

"She didn't mean to betray a confidence. She was just so nervous about how you would feel coming back here that she *had* to talk about it. She's been so concerned about you, Gabriel, you have no idea," Johnson said, and Gabriel felt a wash of guilt run through him.

"There's nothing for her to worry about," Gabriel said softly. He tightened his hold on himself.

"She told me that you blamed yourself for your parents' deaths," Johnson said. "Because you had picked that spot to sail to, and that spot was where the rogue waves appeared that sank the boat."

He *had* blamed himself for that choice. The "what ifs" had haunted him for years. What if he hadn't insisted on going out on the boat that day? What if he had told his father to pick where they sailed? What if they had sailed closer to shore like his mother had wanted? His grandmother hadn't understood his guilt. She had assured him over and over again that it was not his fault, that he could not have known where the storm would be or where the rogue waves would appear. No one could.

But is that true? I'm a Mer with a connection to the sea. Was I sensing something out there in the depths? Did some part of me know—and yearn for—the storm to come so I could ... could see it? It ... something miles high with tentacles ... That thought stopped Gabriel cold. That was madness. That "it" was not real.

"I—I did choose where we went that day," Gabriel found himself saying. "My mother wanted to sail closer to shore. She had heard a weather report that a storm might be coming, but I convinced her that we had to go out farther than she wanted. So ... yes, I *am* responsible for us being there when the storm came."

"What was it about that particular spot that called to you, Gabriel?" Johnson asked. He lowered his voice as if he wanted this to be a secret just between them. "Did you *hear* something coming from there? *Feel* something? *See* something?"

The pull. It was like a silver thread connecting me to that part of the ocean. I had to go there. Nothing could have stopped me from going there. How could Johnson know about that? Again he mentally shook himself. *He doesn't know! He's guessing.*

"I ... I don't know," Gabriel answered, his lips numb.

He had always believed that it was just a childish whim that had made him pick that terrible spot. But what if that wasn't true? What if he had been *compelled* in some way? He passed a shaky hand over his suddenly damp forehead.

"What did you think at the time? What did you *feel*?" Johnson asked.

Gabriel's mouth opened and he heard himself saying, "I just felt—felt that we had to go there, because …"

"Because?" Johnson pressed, and Gabriel could have sworn the older man was holding his breath as he awaited Gabriel's answer.

Because something amazing was going to happen. Something amazing was waiting there. Waiting for me. Something miles high with tentacles.

Gabriel shuddered as he remembered the tentacles rising up from the glittering depths after the boat sank. Another wash of cold sweat broke out on his forehead and upper lip. *That thing couldn't be real*, he told himself for what felt like the millionth time. It was a monster that his oxygen-starved mind had created based on his mother's story about the Mer's Guardian. He hadn't been drawn out to that spot in the ocean because that monstrous creature was there. That was just impossible!

"Gabriel, is everything all right?" Johnson again laid one of his massive hands on Gabriel's shoulder. His thick, dark eyebrows drew together in concern.

"I—I—everything's *fine*," Gabriel got out. He was shaking and felt so ill again.

"You look rather pale. Let me help you," Johnson said. His voice was gentle, but there was a hungry expression in his eyes.

"Help me? You're the last person who could *help* me! You're the one talking about my parents! I don't want to speak about it! Can't you understand that?" Gabriel's voice was shrill. He would never share his thoughts with Johnson. The more eager the older man was to hear them, the less Gabriel wanted to reveal.

He stepped away from Johnson's touch. "Why do you want to drag it all up again? What business is it of yours?"

There was a flash of disappointment, and maybe even frustration, in Johnson's eyes. "You must think it very strange that I'm asking you these questions."

"Strange?! Strange?!" Gabriel crossed his arms over his chest. "More than strange! Sadistic, actually!"

Johnson flinched. He held up one hand as if to placate Gabriel. "I assure you that the *last* thing I want to do is hurt you. I want to *help* you."

"You have a bizarre way of showing it!" Gabriel wanted to go inside. He didn't want to be there any longer, but there was something in Johnson's expression and voice that held him there despite his anger, pain and fear.

"There is a *reason* I'm asking you about all of this. A *good* reason." The older man put his hands on his hips and looked down at his feet. He was quiet for a moment, but then began to speak again. "My last mission in the military took me to a remote jungle island."

"I don't care to hear a *story*—"

Johnson raised one hand again, which silenced Gabriel, and continued, "I swear you will understand my point after I've told you this."

"I don't see why I should stay a second longer with you!"

"Please," Johnson begged. "*Please.*"

Gabriel stared for a long moment at Johnson. His temper wanted him to turn his back on the man. But his instinct told him to stay and listen. "All right. Fine. Tell me then."

"Thank you," Johnson said, letting out a relieved breath.

"Don't thank me. Just say what you have to say," Gabriel said sharply.

Johnson nodded. "All right. Fair enough." He paused, apparently centering himself, and then began, "The military had a listening post on a remote Pacific island. A young man about your

103

age, name of Kane, was stationed on the island two months before—before things went *wrong*." Johnson's gaze went distant as he remembered. "The listening post's main purpose was to keep track of enemy vessels on the sea and intercept their messages, decode them and send them on to the mainland. And Kane was brilliant at it. He seemed to know just where our enemies' ships were at all times, all over the globe. His colleagues joked that he had an *affinity* for water."

Gabriel's stomach fluttered uncertainly. A young man with an affinity for water? That sounded rather familiar. Could Kane have Mer blood, too? "Something happened to him?"

"Something happened to the people *around* him," Johnson said. "I suppose something happened to him, too, but ... but I've always suspected that he survived somehow. I have no proof of it. Just a feeling in my gut."

Survived? Like how I survived drowning twice? Or something else?

Gabriel's back straightened. "What exactly do you think he survived?"

"The first sign of something being wrong at the base came a month after he arrived." Johnson crossed his wrists behind his back as if he were reporting. "Kane claimed that he was hearing signals, *music of the deep*, he later called it. No one else heard what he did. And this music, which he said he traced to the Marianas Trench ... well, it didn't correspond to any human activity."

"So he was tracking fish? Whales? Sharks?" Gabriel's voice sounded high and fake to his own ears. He had a terrible feeling he knew what Kane had been hearing: the Mer. And he hadn't been hearing them over the machines, but from inside his own head.

"No, Gabriel, other people would have heard it too if it was anything like that," Johnson said, his expression stony. "Kane became obsessed with this music of the deep to the exclusion of all else."

"So was he actually hearing something or just going crazy?" Gabriel asked.

Johnson did not answer his question. Instead, he said, "They found Kane destroying all of the listening equipment one night. He was smashing it to bits with a crowbar. He was *raving* that the music wasn't ours to listen to, that we were violating its domain and that we must leave the sea to it." Johnson swallowed. Kane's words obviously still unsettled him to this day. "They locked him up, still screaming. He never stopped screaming. The last message from the base informed us of these developments and then … it went *dark*."

"You mean the base stopped reporting?" Gabriel asked. He was surprised that his voice sounded so even, because his heart was pounding in his chest even though he did not know exactly why.

The sea is "its"? The Mers? But then wouldn't "it" be plural? Them? They? Not "it". And why would the Mers attack a military base anyways? Why not just contact Kane and take him into the water if he was transitioning?

"I was sent in to find out what had happened to the base." Johnson's head lifted and his eyes were bleak. "The station was utterly destroyed. More than destroyed. It was simply *gone*."

That doesn't sound like the Mers. I can't believe Casillus or anyone related to him would order such a thing, or even be able to do such a thing.

Gabriel blinked. "How could a whole station be gone?"

"The only clue about what had happened there was this bizarre *compaction*, an extreme *compression*, of the land." Johnson didn't even blink as he explained, "The compression started far offshore. We followed it from the seabed to the sandy beach and then up to the asphalted area around the base. The ground looked as if something impossibly heavy had *slid* up from the sea, crushed the station beneath its bulk, and then dragged the remains into the deep."

Something miles high with tentacles. Another shudder ran through Gabriel.

"Did you ever figure out what happened?" Gabriel asked faintly.

Johnson's gray eyes gleamed. "I know what caused it, yes. I found reports of it appearing throughout the ages written in esoteric books. Visions of it drawn on crumbling, ancient pages. Horrified whispers of its existence passed down through generations. But no one in the military would believe me. The people at Miskatonic *did*. They had come across this *thing* too, and others, many others, like it or worse. Studying things like this is the university's purpose."

Gabriel didn't ask what the thing was. His mouth wouldn't form the words. Instead, he asked, "Is that why you're a professor at Miskatonic now and not in the military any longer?"

"Yes, Gabriel." Johnson was standing at attention as if he were in military uniform still and not in a robe several sizes too small. "You see, I found that the *best* place I could be to protect this country—all of humanity, actually—was at Miskatonic, *not* in the military."

Protect humanity? From the Mers? Or that thing ...

"Why are you telling me this, Johnson?" Gabriel asked, remembering why Johnson had supposedly begun this story in the first place, which was to explain his interest in Gabriel's parents' deaths.

"I told you this because I *know* that there are things in this world, *forces*, that few people would understand, let alone believe," Johnson said. His gaze was piercing.

"I still don't see what that has to do with me or how my parents died," Gabriel lied.

"Just that I would *believe* you, Gabriel, if you told me that you were *compelled* to go to that particular spot in the ocean that day," Johnson said, his voice almost pleading. "I wouldn't tell you that you were *mistaken* or ... *mad*, like so many others would, if you confessed that to me. I would understand. I would try to help you."

A chill ran through Gabriel. He felt so exposed, so vulnerable. "It seems like you've already made up your mind about what happened that day, Johnson."

"Perhaps I have. But I would like to hear it from you." Johnson paused as if he expected Gabriel to say something, but Gabriel just stared silently back at him. "Since coming to Ocean Side has anything happened? Have you felt *compelled* like you did that day your parents died? Are there *any* strange things happening to you again, Gabriel?" Johnson was so still.

Strange things? Oh, Johnson, you don't know the half of it.

After three beats of silence where all Gabriel could hear was his own frantic heartbeat, he lied, "I have no idea what you're talking about."

"I think you do."

"I'm sorry about Kane and the people at the base, but that has nothing—"

"The thing that destroyed the base … Miskatonic has been tracking it for decades," Johnson said.

"Tracking …" Gabriel's voice dropped off. He found that he was hardly breathing as he waited for Johnson to say more.

"Yes, *tracking*. What drew me most to overseeing the settlement excavation, Gabriel, was that the tracking records showed that *it* had been here. It had been exactly where your boat went down that day. Exactly where your parents died," Johnson said calmly. "It was *there* that *day*."

Gabriel felt like he was going to throw up or fall to the ground and curl into a ball. He did not believe in monsters. He now believed in Mers, but not things miles high with tentacles.

"I—I've got to go," Gabriel mumbled through numb lips.

"I'll be here when you're ready to talk," Johnson said, obviously confident he would be back. "And whatever you say, I'll believe you."

Gabriel turned on his heel and fled for the interior of the house. His heart was beating so hard that it felt like it wanted to

107

escape from his chest. The bitter taste of fear coated the back of his throat. His feet slipped on the steps of the porch and he almost fell. He caught himself at the last moment on the porch's railing. His momentum spun him halfway around, and he caught sight of Johnson behind him.

The older man wasn't rushing after him. He wasn't even looking at Gabriel. Instead, he was staring down at the beach. Specifically, he was gazing at the footsteps Casillus had left in the sand, the footsteps that led into the sea, but did not come back out of it.

If you enjoyed *The Merman – Book 2: Acceptance*, check out another title by X. Aratare, *The Artifact – Book 1: The Bodyguard*.

Sean Harding is a born protector. As a police detective for the wealthy city of Winter Haven, Sean thinks he has found his purpose, but then things go terribly wrong and he loses his partner, his job and even hope. That is until he meets Dane Gareis …

Dane Gareis is a wealthy, reclusive young man with a traumatic past, but a spine of steel. When his father is killed in a mysterious plane crash, Dane carries on the family business and continues his passion for the very antiquity that got his father murdered — a golden sarcophagus belonging to an ancient cult known as the Ydrath.

Soon, the Ydrath threaten him as well, and Dane seeks to hire a bodyguard he can trust. Someone who can protect him, and someone who will respect his boundaries. While he gets the first two, the third requirement falls apart when he hires Sean Harding.

Sparks immediately fly between them. And as it turns out, there is more to connect them than simply a job.

Read the preview of chapter one...

THE ARTIFACT – Book1: The Bodyguard

CHAPTER 1
SOLE SURVIVOR

Detective Sean Harding thrust open Winter Haven Memorial's emergency room doors. He strode past the nurse on duty with a flash of his detective badge and a curt nod. The badge was a necessity. As an undercover operative for the Winter Haven Special Task Force and Narcotics Unit, known simply as "the Unit," he didn't look the part of a police detective even when he wore a suit like today.

His dark brown hair was long enough for it to begin to curl and brush the tops of his shoulders, and he had a perpetual five o'clock shadow. His olive-toned skin spared him from looking vampire-pale despite long hours spent on night-darkened streets and in the windowless rooms of clubs. But despite having been up for over thirty-six hours straight, Sean's green eyes still looked sharp and clear.

He hadn't stopped moving since first hearing about the drug that was known simply as the Powder. Everything surrounding the drug was shrouded in darkness. Where it came from, who was behind its manufacture, and even its actual chemical makeup were all unknown. The only thing that was certain was that it killed everyone who took it. And that fact made Sean fear there would be a holocaust of drug users unless he could locate the source of the Powder and choke off its flow. He had finally gotten his first solid lead tonight in the form of a phone call from Dr. Olga Vostok, a

112

good friend and emergency room physician at Winter Haven Memorial.

"Sean," Dr. Vostok had said. "We have a survivor."

"Are you sure?" His heart rate had risen.

"Yes. He's a young man. More like a boy. He took the Powder and he's here. Alive," she had said, her voice rushed and strained.

"Keep him alive, Olga. If he says anything—I mean ANYTHING, write it down, record it, remember it. Do whatever you have to do," Sean had ordered. As soon as he had hung up, he had jumped into his car, peeled out of the police station's parking lot. He got to the ER in record time.

And now he was here, in the hospital, feet away from the boy that could turn his investigation around. Sean yanked aside the curtain that surrounded the boy's hospital bed. The sound of the metal rings sliding along the pole was nearly deafening. He froze.

Too late.

Sean recognized death when he saw it. His gaze riveted on the red blood oozing out of the corners of the boy's unseeing blue eyes. It looked especially vibrant against the child's chalky white skin. The blood trails were dry, appearing almost painted on in their vividness. For a moment, Sean wanted to grab the boy's shoulders and shake him. He wanted to believe that the red was makeup or paint. But he knew it was not. The boy was dead and gone. Sean swallowed the bile that rose in his throat.

"His brain liquefied. We will need an autopsy to confirm it, but I am sure already. Just like the others," Dr. Vostok's Russian-accented voice suddenly came from behind him. Startled, Sean spun around to face her. His first thought was that she looked as deathly pale as the boy. "Sorry. Didn't mean to scare you, Sean."

Sean waved off her apology even as his heart still thundered in his chest. "How long ago did he die?"

"Moments after I called you, so the guilt in your eyes is unfounded. You couldn't have gotten here in time unless you had teleported." She touched his shoulder tenderly, but he didn't want tenderness. The disappointment was too great.

"He is—*was*—the only lead I had, Olga. More are going to die, because I didn't get here fast enough."

Dr. Vostok walked over to the boy's bed. Her dark blonde hair gleamed under the fluorescent lights. The lines that framed her mouth deepened as she looked down at the dead boy. She lightly placed one of her hands on the child's forearm. Sean noticed that her nails were bitten to the quick.

"He took the Powder just once," she said softly. "Just once, and this was the result. He looks all of fifteen, doesn't he?"

"Any ID?" Sean's police instincts kicked in even as his shoulders slumped in exhaustion and despair. Another lead to nowhere.

"No, no ID. No wallet. He didn't even have on shoes or a shirt when he wandered into the ER," she said, patting the boy's arm.

"Did he say who he bought the drug from?" Sean asked.

She shook her head. "He would only speak of what the drug showed him."

"So it causes hallucinations?" Sean asked wearily. He expected a quick confirmation from Dr. Vostok, but she was silent for so long that Sean began to feel a trickle of unease. "Olga?"

"I don't know," she said, then shook herself. "I mean, most probably. Yes, definitely, it causes hallucinations. He couldn't have really been seeing what he claimed he was. It's quite impossible." The last was said softly, almost as if she were speaking to herself.

Sean grasped her elbow gently. "What is it? You look unnerved. I've never seen you like this."

"Unnerved? That's a very good word to use to describe how I feel." She wrapped her arms around herself as she added, "This drug, Sean, it isn't like anything I've ever seen. If you had heard what he *said*. His voice is still in my mind."

"Tell me," Sean urged.

"He said that I should think of reality as a matryoshka," she said.

"A matryoshka?" Sean asked. The word was alien on his tongue, and didn't sound like something a fifteen-year-old would know.

"It is the Russian term for a traditional Russian nesting doll," she explained. "You know, the wooden dolls where, when you open them, there are other dolls inside."

"Oh, I've seen those." Sean's brow furrowed as his confusion grew with the explanation. "And he used the word 'matryoshka'?"

"Yes, it is strange, isn't it?" Dr. Vostok let out a soft, uneasy laugh. "And what's even stranger is that I believe he used that metaphor just for *me*. Just so that *I* would understand. But if he had been speaking to someone else, he would have used a different metaphor. A metaphor that would have resonated for that person." She wrapped her arms around herself again. "He was dying, Sean. His brain was literally becoming soup in his skull, but he was thinking at such a level—I cannot explain it."

"Did he say anything else about this—this nesting doll metaphor?"

She nodded. "He said that I should imagine that the outermost nesting doll is the world as we know it. That doll is the reality we can see. But the drug, the Powder, has the ability to pull that doll apart and show us what is inside."

"And what does the inside look like?" Sean asked, that earlier trickle of unease becoming a torrent.

"Beautiful and terrible." Dr. Vostok shivered. "He told me that just one layer down from here, just *one*, things get a whole lot more interesting, but if you continue on, you will find ..." She suddenly stopped and let out a nervous little laugh that had the hair on the back of Sean's neck standing on end.

"What do you find?" Sean asked, resisting the urge to shake her. His desperation to know *anything* about the drug rose up in him stronger than ever.

Her eyes were bright, glassy with unspeakable unease, as she said, "You'll find that we're not alone. But having seen who we're sharing all of this with, you'll wish we were."

*****

The full book is available in our shop in ePub, Kindle, PDF, paperback and there is also an audio-book version on Amazon, Audible and iTunes!

PUBLISHING

Raythe Reign Deals & Coupons

Are you in the mood for more dark, sexy m/m stories? Check out our online shop here, where you can find ALL available works from us (some not available on Amazon.)

http://shop.raythereign.com

And if you want to be the first to know about new Raythe Reign releases, join our update list!

We'll send you a note as soon as the next volume is out. People on our update list will also get some insider info...

- Exclusive monthly deals for books and manga through our own shop.
- Coupons for our monthly membership, which has *something new to see or read* every day of the year (even Christmas!)
- Contests, giveaways, and things like AMAs (ask-me-anything sessions.)
- Events we're participating in, such as conventions, discussion panels, etc.
- Progress updates about current series, new series, stories, and side content.

- Exclusive content you can ONLY find through our shop, such as sexy stories and graphic novels that are <u>too hot for Amazon</u> to sell.

Join here: http://shop.raythereign.com/raythe-reign-update-list/

- Raythe Reign Team

24604236R00068

Made in the USA
Middletown, DE
30 September 2015